TROUBLE

ALLYSON JAMES

ELLORA'S CAVE
ROMANTICA PUBLISHING

What the critics are saying...

છ

"James proves two are indeed better than one in this scorching tale of twin demi-gods." *~Romantic Times BOOKReviews*

"A sweet, funny and deliciously erotic read you won't want to miss." *~ Romance Reviews Today*

"A fascinating, mythical, exciting, romantic and erotic tale." *~ Just Erotic Romance Reviews*

"I was thoroughly charmed from the first page of the book." *~ Eromance Reviews*

"In the book...Fiona says to herself, "It's like a fabulous piece of chocolate—you start out with a little taste, a little nibble to sate your craving and tempt yourself at the same time, and then you really dig in. Savor this." This is the perfect summary of Double Trouble." *~ Joyfully Reviewed*

An Ellora's Cave Romantica Publication

www.ellorascave.com

Double Trouble

ISBN 9781419956676
Edited by Heather Osborn
Cover art by Lissa Waitley & Syneca

Electronic book Publication June 2006
Trade paperback Publication June 2007

This book was printed in the U.S.A by Jasmine-Jade Enterprises, LLC.

Content Advisory:

S – ENSUOUS
E – ROTIC
X – TREME

Ellora's Cave Publishing offers three levels of Romantica™ reading entertainment: S (S-ensuous), E (E-rotic), and X (X-treme).

The following material contains graphic sexual content meant for mature readers. This story has been rated E–rotic.

S-*ensuous* love scenes are explicit and leave nothing to the imagination.

E-*rotic* love scenes are explicit, leave nothing to the imagination, and are high in volume per the overall word count. E-rated titles might contain material that some readers find objectionable—in other words, almost anything goes, sexually. E-rated titles are the most graphic titles we carry in terms of both sexual language and descriptiveness in these works of literature.

X-*treme* titles differ from E-rated titles only in plot premise and storyline execution. Stories designated with the letter X tend to contain difficult or controversial subject matter not for the faint of heart.

Also by Allyson James

❧

Christmas Cowboy
Ellora's Cavemen: Dreams of the Oasis I (*anthology*)
Ellora's Cavemen: Seasons of Seduction I (*anthology*)
Tales of the Shareem: Aiden and Ky
Tales of the Shareem: Maia and Rylan
Tales of the Shareem: Rees
Tales of the Shareem: Rio

About the Author

❧

Allyson James began writing at age eight. She wrote love stories before she knew what romances were, dreaming of the day when her books would appear at libraries and bookstores. One day, she, decided to stop dreaming and do it for real.

After a long struggle and inevitable rejections, she at last sold a romance novel, then to her surprise several mystery novels, more romances, and erotic romances to Ellora's Cave, and became a bestselling author. She writes under several pseudonyms, has been nominated for and won Romantic Times Reviewer's Choice awards, and has had starred reviews in Booklist and Top Pick reviews in Romantic Times.

Allyson loves to write, read, hike, and build dollhouses. She met her soul mate when she was eighteen, traveled around the world with him, and settled down with him in the desert southwest.

Allyson welcomes comments from readers. You can find her website and email address on her author bio page at www.ellorascave.com.

DOUBLE TROUBLE

ဢ

Trademarks Acknowledgement

Chapter One

ᔥ

The last shard of the vessel lay in Fiona's hand.

Fiona's sex jar, the other archeologists snickered.

The painting on the terracotta two-handled jar depicted two beautiful men with long, very erect cocks, one on either side of a voluptuous woman.

Their penises half penetrated the woman in profile, one in front, one behind, in an impossible position. The woman hovered between the two, her head thrown back in ecstasy, her long black hair touching the cock of the man behind her.

Their naked male physiques were in excellent shape, their faces near perfect, and each of them had unruly black, curling hair that ended just below the napes of their necks. The painting followed the sinuous curve of the jar and the men's muscular arms nearly touched in the back.

Fiona could study the painting for hours, enjoying the art of that long dead Athenian who had caught the threesome in their erotic act.

The ancient Athenians had not been afraid of sex. Neither was Fiona, but spending her days in a muffled office or digging things out of the dirt under the broiling sun didn't give her much chance to have any. Her last boyfriend had departed three years ago, and now the only time she got on her hands and knees with a man was to help him brush dust from unearthed pottery.

So she looked at the vessel that dated to 500 B.C.E. and wished she were the woman in the middle. She wondered if the painting depicted a myth or just the artist's own fantasy. Maybe someday her research would discover its secret.

Fiona had needed one piece, brilliant red tipped with black, to complete the jar she'd been working on in the Athenian Agora for the past two summers.

Today, almost as if by accident, the last piece had nearly leapt at her from the spread of potsherds in the collection room. Now she held it in her hand, the ancient clay smooth and cool.

At last.

A gray tabby that enjoyed lounging about the site chose that moment to rub Fiona's legs. Used to her by now, Fiona barely jumped at the brush of fur on her bare skin.

She dabbed the shard with the paste they used to glue pots together, and with a satisfied smile, carefully set the last piece into place.

A sudden vibration hummed through her body. She heard a loud click, and the lights went out.

Someone outside the pottery room groaned. "Generator's gone again. To hell with it, I'm going to bed."

Fiona took out her pocket flashlight and made her way to the door. The offices were in complete darkness, but no one panicked—everyone was used to the temperamental generator. Mostly they muttered swear words and left the building.

Fiona left too, the cat staying behind in the comfortable dark. Fiona headed back to the dorm and the tiny private bedroom awarded her because she was a postdoc, a small step up from the graduate students who bunked four together in one-room apartments spread throughout the city.

She sighed as she crossed the compound under the mild Athens night. Such an anticlimactic end to a day she'd looked forward to for two years. She'd finished her jar, but no one very much cared except herself.

The true life of an archeologist, she thought with an inward laugh. *No Indiana Jones adventures for me.*

* * * * *

In the pottery room, unseen by anyone but the gray cat who watched the jar with intense yellow eyes, the black and red vessel began to rock. A wisp of smoke rose from the top, the crazed cracks of the pieced-together shards vanished and the painted figures began to glow…

* * * * *

Fiona woke to whispers.

"Think she'll be as beautiful when she opens her eyes?" It was a masculine voice, deep and rich and slightly accented. Greek.

"Have you ever seen hair this color? It is like the depths of fire." The second voice was just as deep, just as rich, just as sinfully sexy.

"Is it real, do you think?"

"It's like the finest gossamer woven by Ariadne." Fiona felt faint touch in her hair then it was gone.

"What language are we speaking?" the first man asked.

"English."

"Never heard of it."

"It must be her language," the second man said. "Of course we'd understand it. She's obviously a great sorceress." Again the faint touch in her hair. "And a beautiful one."

"I saw her first."

"The fuck you did. We arrived at the same time."

Fiona lay still, wondering what kind of dream had taken over her tired brain. She felt a warm weight on either side of her, as though the men had stretched out on the narrow bed with her. Musky and masculine scents wove through her half-asleep mind, soothing and comforting.

Their voices were similar, but she sensed a difference. The first man sounded amused, as though he found the world perpetually funny. The second had a poetic turn, rich syllables sliding from his tongue in beautiful phrases.

"I wonder where we are," the first one said. "Last thing I remember is that bitch in the temple, and then—nothing."

"It is too dark. Is she a goddess, do you think?"

"Her fingers are dirty."

Fiona felt her hand being raised and a brush of something warm—lips—across her fingertips. She stirred, the space between her legs heating.

"A goddess can get her fingers dirty if she wants to," the second man said, his voice deep and warm.

What a magnificent dream.

Fiona's eyelids began to open, and she fought waking up. *Stay asleep, enjoy it.* Waking up would bring dull reality rushing back.

Sure, spending her summers in Athens working in the ancient ruins was exotic, but only until the lights didn't work and the plumbing backed up, and a peanut butter sandwich seemed like food of the gods.

Fiona's eyelids wouldn't cooperate. They slid open and her eyes took in the darkness of the room.

Except the dream didn't go away. Two large, hard-bodied men lay full-length on either side of her, each propped up on one elbow, each with black hair rumpled to the napes of their necks. Two faces of hard, identical handsomeness hung over hers, two pairs of glittering dark eyes fixed on her.

Twins, she thought distractedly.

Both men were stark naked. They lay languorously on her bedcovers, legs stretched to entwine with hers, sculpted pectorals dusted with black hair, arms raw with muscle. The one on her left had her hand in his and was brushing his lips over her fingers.

The one on her right looked at her with such intense concentration that his gaze seemed to bore straight through her head.

She opened her mouth to scream but only a strangled dry sound came out.

"Shh," said the one holding her hand, his breath tickling her skin.

For some reason, she wanted to obey him instead of fighting her way free and shouting for help.

"Are you a sorceress?" the one on her right asked softly. "Or a goddess?"

Fiona gulped. "Neither. I'm…an archaeologist."

The two men exchanged a glance. "*Ar-chaeo-lo-gist*," the man on her right said, lips carefully pronouncing the syllables. "A Greek word. Studier of the past?"

"Yes. I guess so." At the moment, Fiona was not sure exactly what she did. "Who the hell are you, and what are you doing in my room?"

The two men looked at each other, surprised. "You freed us," said the one on her right, his intense look deepening.

"We were drawn to you," the first man said, his lips lingering on her fingertips. "After the spell broke and you freed us. Of course we want to thank you."

The second man's smile changed his serious demeanor. "We will thank you in whatever way you like." He laid his hand across her abdomen and even through the blankets, his large palm soaked heat into her.

"Wait." Fiona struggled to sit up. "I freed you? From what? I've never seen you before. I haven't been anywhere but the dig in weeks. You're mistaking me for someone else."

"No," the first one said.

They started speaking at the same time, each finishing the other's sentences. "We were trapped—"

"In oblivion—"

"For eternity."

"It seemed like eternity."

"Do you know how boring oblivion is?"

"Especially with *him*."

They glared at each other. "At least I know more than two jokes," the one on her right said.

"At least I don't sing. Zeus above, but your voice would make a Hydra cringe."

Fiona waved her hands to break in. "Oblivion?"

Their banter ceased, smiles vanishing. "It was dark—"

"And so damn cold."

"Lonely."

"The dark could eat your soul."

They stopped.

Fiona hugged her knees to her chest, aware she wore only a thin nightshirt over her rather ample curves. The sadness in their voices pulled at her, but she had to remember that two naked strangers had broken into her room and gotten into bed with her, and what she really should do is get away from them and run for security.

But they were so compelling. Their features were nearly identical and yet not. The man to her left had a twinkle in his eyes that the one on her right did not, and his lips creased into ready smiles while his brother was more serious.

But the man on her right had such a compelling gaze that she found herself swaying toward him when he spoke.

"At least tell me who you are," she said faintly.

"Pollux," said the man on her left side.

"Castor," said the man on her right.

"Castor and Pollux?" Fiona repeated. "Like the Greek demigods? Like the Gemini constellation?"

Pollux nodded, his easy smile wide. "That's us."

She shot a glance at Castor, who also nodded.

"Good lord," she spluttered. "Your mother named you after a constellation?"

They looked puzzled. "The constellation was named for us," Castor said. "Our mother was Leda."

"She had a partiality to swans," Pollux grinned. "Don't tell her husband."

"Swans." Fiona dragged in a breath. "You mean Leda and the swan. Leda and *Zeus*."

"Yes," Castor said.

So — they're tall, dark, handsome and insane. "Leda was the mother of Helen of Troy," she said faintly.

They both nodded.

"Our sister," Pollux said. "People can get up to the stupidest things. An entire civilization destroyed because of a cuckolded husband's pique."

Fiona held up both hands. "All right, just stop. I won't report you or call the police if you simply leave my room and get out of the compound. Really. You go, I don't say a word, and you never come back."

The two men looked at each other.

"She's afraid of us," Castor said, in a tone of surprise.

"But you freed us," his brother said. "You must have known when you broke the spell that we'd devote ourselves to you. No one fears Castor and Pollux. We're the demigods of good times."

"And duality," Castor said softly. "Identical, yet completely different. Those born under our influence have a great capacity for art."

"And discourse," Pol added.

"For Greek demigods, you speak English very well," Fiona pointed out.

"Because it is your language," Castor said. "The magic that brought us back allows us to understand it."

"Oh. Right."

Pollux unfolded himself from the bed. The room was still dark, the moonlight leaking through the thin curtains not enough to illuminate them completely, but she could see that Pollux was tall, well over six feet. Every muscle on his torso rippled in perfect harmony.

"What do you want us to do to prove we're who we say we are?" he asked.

"You can't," she said at once.

Castor took advantage of his brother's absence to move closer to her. Something large and firm pressed her thigh, a satin prod against her bare skin. *His cock.* She could see only Pollux's upper torso in the dark, but knew that he was just as naked and his cock must be just as large.

Her heart beat swiftly, the part of her that was all woman waking up and taking notice.

Castor smoothed a lock of hair with his broad fingers. "Why do you not believe us?"

Should you argue with crazy people or just go along with what they say?

Fiona dragged in a breath. "Castor and Pollux—the Gemini twins—it's all a myth, made up thousands of years ago. By people with no concept of genetics, by the way, because if I remember right, Castor and Pollux had different fathers, and you can't have identical twins with different fathers. People thought that about women with twins—that they'd cheated on their husbands—because, like I said, they didn't know anything about genetics."

Her words ran out as her mouth dried and breath deserted her. She realized that both men were staring at her like she was the one who was crazy.

"Thousands of years," Pollux repeated.

"Yes."

Castor looked troubled. "How many thousands?"

"I don't know. Troy was what, five or six thousand years ago? You must have been born about twenty or so years before that, right?"

Silence fell. The night was quiet, the only sounds a distant hum of a car and the scuttle of claws from the mice they could never get rid of.

When Castor spoke, his voice was subdued. "We did not know that much time had passed."

"It was so cold," Pollux repeated. He folded his arms across his broad chest, flexing muscles that any other time Fiona would be thrilled to watch. And touch and lick...

Fiona felt their distress and for some reason wanted to comfort her crazy naked men. "You're all right now," she began.

Castor gave her a warm look. "Yes, because of you. Our strong sorceress to break the spell."

"It was strong magic," Pollux added. "I sensed that even as Selena made the vessel and started to pull us in. We have strong magic but we could not resist. It bound us fast."

"She laughed at us," his brother finished. "Said the great Castor and Pollux would be nothing but faces on a jar."

Fiona's eyes widened. "Jar?"

She finally fought free of the covers and scrambled to her feet.

"I know what this is all about. They sent you, didn't they? Bob and Joan Whittington. They've made fun of my sex jar from day one, but they're pretty annoyed I got that huge write-up in *Archaeology Today* and especially *National Geographic*. They scorn popular publications, but at the same time, they were pissed as hell. They sent you, didn't they? As a big joke. They must have found out I finished the vessel."

Both men looked blank. Castor and Pollux—if that were their names, which she doubted—exchanged a puzzled glance.

She put her hands to her head, tugging at her tousled hair. "Oh God, if they've done anything to the jar..."

She snatched a pair of jeans from a chair and jammed her feet in the dusty sneakers she kept by the door. Without looking back at the two men, she grabbed her flashlight, slammed out of her room and hastened to the pottery room. Thankfully, no one saw her and she was able to dash into the room alone, shut the door and turn on the light.

The generator must have been reset because the electric lamp above the worktable glowed readily when she turned the switch. The gray cat, which had curled itself into a ball underneath the table, raised its head and blinked at her.

The vessel sat where she'd left it. Except it had completely changed.

Gone were the cracks that showed where the pieces had been fitted together. The painting likewise had altered. The two identical men—Castor and Pollux?—had changed position.

They were now standing back to back, arms folded over well-muscled chests, cocks still rampant. The woman had disappeared completely, leaving a blank space of red terracotta between them.

Chapter Two

ℰ

Cas eased himself from the bed and told his inflated cock to go down.

The sorceress, their rescuer, was beautiful, her body all curves and valleys, a voluptuous playground for his hands. He'd fallen instantly in love with her round, sweet face and her fire-colored hair like warm silk.

He'd hoped that easing her awake would result in a long bout of love-play. He'd wanted to slide her thin garment from her and explore her body with gentle fingers. He'd scented her desire as she moved between them, a woman aroused even under her fear and indignation.

Her anger made no sense. If she had released them from the vessel and Selena's spell, why did she seem unhappy to see them?

But she hadn't been completely unhappy. Her nipples had pearled behind her garment and her juices had run warmly between her legs, he had sensed it.

Pol wanted her too. He was darkly erect, his eyes filled with frustrated need. Cas and Pol often shared women—for some reason women liked being pleasured by two men who looked just alike. But Cas felt a pull of possessiveness for the red-haired sorceress and wondered if he and Pol would have a rivalry for her.

"What's the matter with her?" Pol asked.

"She is frightened."

"Why should she be frightened of us? A good wine, a good fuck and we're happy."

"Let us follow her," Cas suggested. "If there are those who would play tricks on her, she will need our protection."

"I'm all for that. Where did she go?"

"Not far. I can scent her. We should move without being seen."

Pol agreed, and the twins invoked their ability to slide between the very air itself to move quickly and undetected.

Cas was relieved to find they still had this skill. He didn't like the idea that they'd been trapped in the vessel for *thousands* of years.

Anything could have happened during that time — the gods overthrown, their powers stripped. Zeus had once overthrown Kronos and the Titans, what was to say that Zeus himself hadn't suffered a downfall and that Cas and Pol would be in danger?

It's all a myth, she'd said. What that meant, Cas did not know, but it did not sound good.

They found their sorceress in a room crammed with shelves and shelves of dusty pieces of clay and ceramics. Each piece had a little card next to it with writing on it. A worktable stood in the middle of the room with a single glowing lamp over it, a cat calmly washing its face underneath.

The worktable was like nothing Cas had ever seen. It had a very smooth surface, but it was not made of wood or marble. Slim metal instruments were lined up carefully on a tray and a few oddly shaped pieces of metal stood nearby in positions of readiness.

Their sorceress stood in front of the table, staring open-mouthed at the jar that sat in prominent position on the table's surface.

Pol sucked in his breath. Cas likewise felt a twinge of uneasiness. It was the amphora, the one the demon demigoddess had made to wreak her revenge on them. It was whole, unbroken.

Cas leaned forward and touched it.

Alerted to their presence, their sorceress jumped and swung around, her brown eyes round. "What did you do to it?"

Cas frowned, not understanding.

Pol rested his hand on the table, looking troubled. "Where did *she* go?"

A good question. If Cas and Pol were free, then Selena might also be free and alive to continue her vengeance.

Cas had no doubt that the red-haired sorceress who'd just freed them—the archaeologist—was powerful, but she'd need protection against Selena, a half-demon demigoddess with a temper.

"Are archaeologists more powerful sorceresses than most?" he asked.

Their goddess wasn't listening. "What are you trying to do, make me a laughingstock? I worked so hard on this…"

Her words cut off at the sound of the door opening behind them. Cas signaled to Pol, and they made themselves *unseen*. Their sorceress, on the other hand, whirled around and clapped her hand over her mouth, suppressing a scream.

The woman who came in the door was nowhere near as beautiful as theirs. She was perhaps twice their sorceress's age and her skin was weathered by the sun. She dressed in clothes that bared her arms and legs, and her graying hair was cropped short.

The woman stared at their sorceress then broke into a laugh. "Fiona, can't you leave that thing alone for ten minutes? Next thing we know you'll be sleeping with it."

Their sorceress — *Fiona*, beautiful name — faced the intruder. She darted a glance to either side of her and didn't see Cas and Pol, which seemed to both relieve and worry her.

"Joan," she said in a breathless voice. "You know I'd never deliberately do anything to harm your work or your husband's. Ever. Professional rivalry is one thing but sabotage is wrong. I would never do such a thing." Her voice held tears.

"I agree," the woman called Joan said. "That's why I came back to find you. Bob and I and Dr. Wheelan went out to a taverna when the generator died, and I thought you might like to join us. The wine isn't particularly good at this one, but after a couple of glasses you stop caring."

Fiona stared at the woman in surprise and suspicion. "That's the only reason you came back?"

"Yes, why else?"

"Not to take pictures or anything?"

Joan looked bewildered. "Pictures of what? Are you feeling all right? You've been working very hard. Exhaustion isn't helpful on a dig."

"And you haven't touched my jar?"

Joan gave her an odd look. "Not everyone in the world is interested in your pottery, Fiona. I have the bronzes I found, you have your jar o' hunky men. I call it square."

Fiona deflated. "Oh."

"I changed my mind. You shouldn't come out with us, you should get some sleep. Ask Dr. Wheelan for a few days sick time. You look terrible."

Shaking her head and without waiting for answer, the woman Joan turned and left the room, clicking the door closed behind her.

Fiona sagged and Cas caught her in his strong arms.

For a minute, he forgot about the vessel and the demon demigoddess Selena and the thousands of years of blank time, and basked in the soft armful Fiona made. Her leggings rubbed nicely against his rising cock, and her curves fit sweetly against his body.

She stared up at him, eyes stark in her white face. "You know, you *really* can't run around the dig naked."

"No one will see us," Cas assured her.

Beyond her Pol lifted the vessel in his hands. "This might be a problem." He sighed and set the jar carefully down. "Or not. Keep this well for us, will you Fiona? I fear what would happen if it came into the wrong hands. Or shattered." He shot Cas a worried look.

"Fiona's magic will protect us." Cas slid his hand to the curve of her waist.

Her red lips parted. "Remind me which of us is crazy again."

Pol rested his hands lightly on his hips. "The Joan-woman is right. You need rest, sweet Fiona. The best thing to do is return to bed."

Cas' pulse sped. "Bed, yes. Let us take care of you."

"I can rub your feet." Pol moved to the other side of her, his grin widening. "Cas will start at your head, and we will meet in the middle."

Fiona gaped, and Cas felt her body temperature rise. She wanted them, he knew it.

But she pushed herself away from Cas and glared at them both. "No you won't. You will leave me alone. You will go away, back wherever you came from—Athens, the constellations, to Bob and Joan's friends—whatever. I will go to bed *by myself* and when I wake up in the morning, everything will be all right."

Her voice was brittle, as though she was trying to convince herself rather than them.

Pol's grin didn't diminish. "We will protect you as you sleep."

She uttered a little scream, fists balled. "Fine. Do what you want. Good night."

She swung around and banged out the door, slapping her hand against the wall as she went. The light above them suddenly went out.

Pol and Cas looked at each other in the dark. "She has power over light," Pol said. "Her magic is great."

Fiona suddenly appeared in the doorway, her rage reaching all the way across the room. "It isn't magic, it's a light switch." She stared at them a moment, then gave her little scream again and hurried away.

Cas and Pol went after her for her protection, but first they paused for about ten minutes to learn the magic of this *light switch*, while the cat watched with apparent glee.

* * * * *

Fiona did not get her peaceful night's sleep alone. By the time she'd flung off her jeans and crawled back into bed, burying her head beneath the covers, the twins returned. She remained motionless under the blankets, for some reason believing they'd disappear if she paid no attention to them.

But that was impossible, because they started playing with the light switch, flipping the overhead light off and on and off and on and off and... Then they started arguing about who got to flip the switch next.

Fiona flung off the covers and rose to her knees on the mattress. "Would you *please* leave it alone!"

The brothers stared at her, still absolutely and gorgeously naked. In the glare of the lamp, she saw every inch of them, broad shoulders, tapered waists, taut thighs, asses to make any woman, even a dried-up pottery specialist, drool.

Their black and curling hair swept back from their foreheads to the napes of necks. Their black eyes smoldered, Pol's with wicked humor, Cas' with something deeper and darker.

They were the spitting image of the men on the red and black vessel, down to their very large and beautiful cocks.

But they couldn't be. Could they?

Maybe she *had* gone out with Joan and Dr. Wheelan, drunk too much ouzo and was dreaming all this.

Cas snapped the light off one last time. He came to the bed, Pol on the other side. "Fiona is right. She must sleep."

He held the covers for her and told her to lie down. Fiona did, too tired now for arguing and worrying and wondering. Gently, Cas shook the covers out over her, smoothing them, his hand soothing through the blankets.

He and Pol climbed back on the bed and lay on either side of her as they had before. Their bodies warmed her, making her relax against her will. Pol's hand moved to her thigh at the same time Cas pressed at kiss to the line of her hair.

"Rest, sweet Fiona," he breathed.

"We will care for you," Pol murmured.

Fiona's eyes closed against her will, and to her surprise she started to drift off to sleep.

Cas began to hum a tune she'd never heard low in his throat. It seemed *ancient* somehow, not music of her own century.

Pol joined in, his voice lending a haunting harmony to his brother's. Under the influence of this music and their light touch, she fell deeply asleep.

When she awoke, Cas and Pol had vanished, the sun was high and Joan Whittington was knocking on her door. Fiona dragged on her jeans again and opened it.

"Dr. Wheelan is looking for you," Joan said, looking smug. "Two men have turned up, saying they're friends of yours from Athens. You little vixen. No wonder you've been looking so tired."

* * * * *

Sure enough, Castor and Pollux were out in the Agora, both talking avidly with Dr. Wheelan. At least, thank God, they'd found clothes.

Both wore jeans slung low on their hips and thin sandals easily obtainable in the flea markets. Pol's t-shirt, stretched tight over his chest, bore the logo of the American School of Classical Studies in Athens. Cas had wrapped a white and blue striped Greek blanket over his torso like a serape.

Dr. Wheelan was in what Fiona recognized as full archaeological-fever mode and didn't seem to notice what either twin wore. Every woman on the dig, Fiona saw, made excuses to walk close to where the three men stood.

"Ah, Fiona," Dr. Wheelan said when he caught sight of her.

He waved her over, looking in no way like he was about to give her a stern, fatherly lecture. "I didn't know you had friends so familiar with the ancient Agora. They have so many ideas, it's just amazing. Why haven't I met you at conferences or read any of your papers?"

"Papers?" Pol asked blankly.

"They're amateurs," Fiona jumped in. "Not associated with any university or group."

"Well, they certainly are knowledgeable. Whose work have you studied?"

Cas gave him a warm smile. "So many people. We live here, you see. It is home to us."

Dr. Wheelan took this at face value. "Strange I haven't seen you any other season. I've been coming here for twenty years."

"We dislike interfering," Cas said.

"Castor and Pollux," Dr. Wheelan chuckled. "So amusing."

"That's us," Pol said.

Dr. Wheelan clasped his hand and shook it hard, a ritual Pol looked upon in surprise. "Stay and look around as much as you like. I don't have any funding to hire extra people, but knowledgeable volunteers are always welcome. Fiona will show you what to do. Right, Fiona?"

"Of course," Fiona said faintly.

"Fine to have met you. We must talk again. Now I have to go calm down another government representative. Makes me wish I was a postdoc again with nothing to do but scrabble in the dirt."

Still talking, he moved off to face the unpleasant duties of administration, leaving Fiona standing before the twins' intense scrutiny.

"What were you telling him?" she demanded.

Pol grinned. "Where everything is. It's been a long time, but I remember this place." He gestured to a depression where a doorway had once existed. "Over there was Praxos' wine shop, not very good wine but good company. Remember the time someone accused him of having another man's wife, and Praxos nearly drowned him in a wine barrel? It was true—Praxos was having it off with the other man's wife *and* the accuser's wife at the same time." He laughed hard.

Cas smiled in memory and then both trailed off.

"Everything's gone," Pol said, his voice suddenly quiet. "Nothing left but dust and bones."

His words tugged at Fiona's heart. She wasn't sure she believed that Cas and Pol were demigods from her vessel brought back to life after twenty-five hundred years, but their sadness in viewing the Agora, the ancient marketplace, was real.

She knew what it was like to return to a place that contained fond memories only to find the building abandoned or torn down to make way for a mall.

Great, now she was feeling sorry for her crazy men.

"The archaeologists are preserving the past," she explained. "We work to understand exactly how everything was and tell everyone about it so it will never be entirely gone. We make sure the world knows and understands the history."

The brothers surveyed the ruins, hands on hips. Cas' eyes were somber. "Even the archeologists' magic cannot restore what has been lost."

"Is the entire world in ruins?" Pol looked up at the crumbling columns of the Acropolis standing on its flat bluff high above the city. "With only the archaeologists to live in it?"

"Of course not," Fiona said. "Athens is huge and thriving, and there are plenty of towns in Greece and its islands. Not to mention the rest of the world."

"Do they have wine shops?" Pol asked.

The sudden hope in his eyes amused her. "Plenty."

Pol exchanged a glance with Cas. "Good." He started to stride away and Cas, after winking at Fiona, followed.

"Wait a minute, where are you going?"

Cas spun around. "To find life. To see Athens thrive."

Alarm trickled through her. She imagined Cas and Pol strolling through Athens, smiling their devastating smiles and proclaiming they were demigods to everyone they met.

She took two steps forward, mouth open to call out. The gray cat from the pottery room took the opportunity to twine itself about her ankles and the mundane feeling brought her to her senses.

Why should Fiona worry about them? They'd broken into her room and refused to leave, and they must have sabotaged her jar.

That was the only explanation she could think of for the change in the painting. They'd stolen the real jar and substituted this fake. Why they should do this, she had no idea, and she really didn't have the energy right now to puzzle it out.

So why should she care if they wandered around Athens by themselves in clothes they likely stole?

They looked so good in the clothes, though. She cocked her head to study them. Every female in range would turn in their tracks as they passed, hoping for one glance from their molten eyes. The women would follow the twins around and every man in town would be after their blood.

Their own fault for being so sexy. Fiona watched them walk away, backsides cupped lovingly in tight jeans, bodies tall, curling hair blue-black under the sun. They were overfull of confidence and about to go out and play in traffic.

She suddenly caught sight of Swedish archeologist Hans Jorgensen on his way to start his daily work. Hans was the only man on the site who came close to Cas and Pol in size. Tall and blond and in great physical shape, he was the official hunk of the dig. In fact, a photographer last year had asked him to pose for a calendar entitled *The He-Men of Archaeology*. Hans had done it, thinking it a good joke.

It suddenly occurred to her that the jeans and shirt Cas and Pol were now walking away in looked suspiciously like the clothes Hans normally favored.

"Damn," she muttered. "I'm going to hate myself for this, I really am."

"Fiona?" Hans stopped and stared at her with his fine blue eyes. "What is this you say?"

Fiona snapped her attention to him. "Nothing. Just talking to myself." She shot him a feeble smile, stepped over the cat and scuttled off after Cas and Pol, who had already vanished around the corner into the city of Athens.

Chapter Three

ဆာ

Cas gazed around in astonishment as they strode through the city. The ruins of the Agora had saddened him, but this new Athens was a cacophony of color and sound that surpassed imagination.

Pol was just as impressed. "Holy mother goddess," he said.

Here and there Cas caught glimpses of old Greece, crumbling walls of stone and roped-off areas containing a forlorn column or two. The Acropolis reared above the city, crowned with the temple to Athena that Pericles had erected not long before Cas and Pol had been trapped in the painting.

But what Cas mostly saw were monoliths that rose into the sky in all different shapes, sizes and colors. And the vehicles—they moved faster than the best-made chariot pulled by the swiftest horses, and there were so many of them.

The vehicles emitted a strange-smelling smoke and sounds louder than anything he'd ever heard. Once in a while the people sitting inside them would wave their arms or shout swear words out of the windows at other vehicles, a ritual that seemed to be common.

The streets wound narrowly through the city, sometimes filled with people on foot, sometimes dominated by the wheeled vehicles. Cas and Pol flowed along with the foot traffic, stopping when they stopped for the vehicles, moving with them when they moved again.

Cas scrutinized the others with interest. The men and boys looked the same as men and boys of centuries past, either walking purposefully or strolling along looking into shop windows and stopping to talk at length to other men.

The women, on the other hand, were much different. In the Athens of the past, respectable ladies stayed at home and never went out. That didn't mean Cas and Pol hadn't found their way *inside* plenty of times, but the only women allowed on the streets had been slaves, very elderly women and courtesans.

These women, walking with heads high, wore everything from the blue leggings similar to what the twins wore to colorful body-hugging dresses that nicely exposed legs and arms. He didn't think the scantily dressed women were courtesans, because they lacked the practiced come-hither looks of professional ladies. These were normal wives and daughters enjoying a walk in the morning sun.

All very strange. But Cas was a demigod who'd lived for centuries, and he'd witnessed changes in fashion and the way in which men and women treated one another. Spartan women, for example, had been very different from the Athenians. Athletic and beautiful, Spartan woman had been more or less ignored by their men and hadn't minded a little seduction by their favorite demigod twins.

Fiona was different from the women of ancient times, but she was also different from the women who walked these streets. The Athenian women he saw now carefully dressed their hair and had every piece of clothing in place.

Fiona's shirt had been buttoned wrong, her short leggings had been worn and dirty at the hem, and she'd scraped her mussed red hair carelessly back into a tail. Cas found her adorable. When he and Pol returned from exploring this new Athens, he would put his arms around her and show her just how adorable he thought she was.

Turning a corner, Cas and Pol found themselves in a sea of market stalls crammed every which way along a square, thronged with men and women from the young in tight clothing to the elderly in black shawls.

The sudden wall of color and sound brought a smile to his face. This was more like it. Here was the world of the Agora brought to life with all its smells and sounds—smoke from roasting meat, squawks of chickens and other fowl, crackling music and off-beat singing, shouts of men and women hawking their wares, the pungent odor of fruit and the green scent of vegetables. Children ran about screaming, mothers shouting after them.

Other non-Greek people were there too, staring as avidly as Cas and Pol. A pretty young woman herded a group like a shepherdess, saying in a loud voice, "The flea market borders the ancient Athenian Agora, which housed not only shops and markets but government and law offices, the mint for coining money, and the prison."

Cas listened with interest as she described the ancient *stoa* or arcaded shops that had traded olives, wine, grain and oil, as well as exotic treasures from the far-flung Persian empire and Egypt. The group shuffled away, staring at the modern flea market, which also held exotic treasures in abundance.

Pol had moved to a booth selling baklava, a pastry sticky with honey and ground pistachios. Cas asked for one and the pungent drink the stall owner called *coffee*.

Cas felt in the pockets of the leggings he'd liberated from the blond man and found a few coins, which he passed to the stall owner. It seemed to be enough, because the stall owner smiled and gave them no coins in return.

Cas and Pol moved through the market, chewing baklava, licking fingers coated with honey. Cas was beginning to like this time, whenever it was. The shoppers seemed relaxed and happy, the sun was hot, no one was pushed aside to make way for the aristocracy and there seemed to be no slaves.

Athens, of course, had always been the leader of the world and this might be the only oasis in a howling wilderness. Time would tell.

Pol soon found a taverna and ducked inside, calling for wine. The proprietor seemed surprised and not ready to open and serve them, but Pol spoke to him for a time, and he agreed. Pol was not above using his powers on people to make them do as he liked.

As the twins settled down with a bottle between them, other men drifted into the taverna and took seats. Pol requested the best wine for them as well.

By the end of the hour, the taverna had filled, the clientele all new friends of Pol and Cas. One man brought out a stringed instrument and soon there was music and clapping and singing.

The proprietor carried another bottle of wine to the table. Next to it he set a small slip of paper with numbers on it.

Cas lifted it the paper between his fingers. "What is this?" he asked in Greek.

The proprietor grinned. "It is what you owe."

Cas felt in his pockets for more coins but found none. Pol had a few paper notes that meant nothing to either of them. The proprietor took the notes but said they needed more.

"We have no more," Pol said. "Are you saying that Castor and Pollux, the sons of Zeus, have to pay for their wine?"

The proprietor laughed loudly. "Dionysus himself would have to pay, my friend. My wife does the accounts."

The entire room went off into hilarity. Pol lifted his cup in salute. "Tell Dionysus to come then. He can pay."

Cas shook his head. "Remember how angry he was last time you did that?"

"True," Pol agreed. "What can we give you, good man? Blessings on your wine and your children? Each will improve tenfold and your taverna will never be empty." Pol drained his cup to cheers from the crowd.

The proprietor reached fingers to the folded-leather pouch Cas had pulled from his pocket and plucked a thin card from its interior. "No problem. I will take this."

He disappeared behind his counter as Cas poured more wine. When the proprietor returned, he handed Cas the card and another slip of paper, then gave him a stylus. "Sign here."

Cas studied the stylus curiously. One end was blunt, bad for marking in wax, and the pointed end was too round. He pressed the pointed end onto the paper, but it made no indentation. He found to his amazement that when he lifted the stylus away it left behind a mark.

He showed Pol, moving the stylus and making lines. The proprietor started to look worried. "I need you to sign the receipt," he said.

Cas picked up the shiny card the proprietor had returned to him and looked at the letters on it. They were not Greek, but whatever magic Fiona had used to bring him and Pol back from oblivion allowed him to read it.

He pressed the stylus to the paper again and copied *Hans Jorgensen.*

This was evidently the correct thing to do, because the proprietor beamed a smile at him, took the slip and went away.

The Athens of this day was obviously a prosperous place, so prosperous that the people could give away their wares and wines freely. All you had to do was give the smooth, thin card to the shop owners and they let you have whatever you wanted. It was astonishing.

Pol and Cas left the taverna to shouts of thanks and farewells and moved through the winding, narrow streets. They walked along, observing everything, out to wider streets with more of the rushing vehicles on them.

As they hesitated on a street corner, wondering where to go next, a small wheeled conveyance pulled to a halt. "Taxi?" the man inside asked.

They stared at him, wondering what he meant.

"You gents want to go somewhere?" the man went on in Greek. "I know the best taverna in Athens. I can take you there."

Pol grinned and clapped Cas on the shoulder. "Excellent. We will see this taverna, and if it is truly the best, we will fetch Fiona and give her wine."

"A good plan," Cas agreed.

The man inside had to get out and show them how the mysterious doors operated. Once Cas and Pol had stuffed themselves into the tiny seat, their long legs folded with knees high, the man hopped back in and the conveyance sped them away at sickening speed.

Cas held up the thin card. "I have this," he said.

The driver grinned at him in a mirror hanging from the window. "Good for you. My friend at the taverna, he will give you all you need."

* * * * *

The demigoddess Selena, spawned from the mating of a god and a wild demon, woke on a hard floor. For a moment, the daylight stunned her and then she realized.

I am outside the jar. The spell is broken.

Well, shit.

She sat up, fuming. Those two damn walking cocks, Cas and Pol, must have tricked her. She was supposed to be with them in that jar for eternity, having sex on top of sex — she'd made sure they couldn't escape.

Except all had been cold darkness, not ecstasy. So much time seemed to pass and yet none at all.

Selena gingerly climbed to her feet, touching her head that pounded with a hell of a migraine. She tried to banish it and couldn't, which pissed her off.

She was a half-demon, half-goddess, why couldn't she get rid of a little headache?

And why couldn't she figure out where the hell she was?

She was in a building, in a room that looked unused. Empty shelves rested against a wall, wooden and broken. A shutter had been latched over a small window.

Selena opened the shutter then jumped back as a strange vehicle roared past, belching fumes.

What demon was this? And could he help her?

She craned to look out of the window, but the strange-smelling demon had gone. Below her was a little alley full of trash. She wrinkled her nose and turned to try the door behind her. It was locked.

That wouldn't do. She rattled the doorknob then stood back and tried to use her magic to heat the lock until it melted.

A wave of weakness hit her and the lock remained intact. *Damn.*

The spell must have drained her more than she'd thought, or else Cas and Pol had found a way to castrate her magic.

Bastards. As soon as she found them, she'd castrate *them* in the literal sense. They had no business being so fucking gorgeous and then deigning to refuse when she invited them to screw her.

Fucking assholes.

Selena pounded on the door. "Let me out of here!" she screamed.

Her language sounded strange to her. It was Greek, but different, as though the words and tones had subtly changed while she was stuck on the jar with the sexy but elusive twins.

In a few moments a key rattled in the lock, and a man stuck his head around the door. He stopped in shock when he saw her.

Selena supposed it would give anyone a shock — finding a voluptuous, naked woman with black hair snaking around her in a locked room must be the highlight of this man's day.

He wasn't bad looking, either. She ran an assessing gaze over him — in his twenties, black hair, brown eyes, tanned skin, well-honed body. She put her hands on her hips and swayed toward him.

"Thank you. I thought I'd be stuck in here forever."

"Uh…" the man said. "How did you get in here?"

"Long story." She hooked her fingers around the man's shirt and pulled him inside, banging the door shut. "I've been in oblivion forever and it's made me really horny. Fuck me."

His brown eyes widened. "What?"

"I said *fuck me*. Has the meaning of the word changed?"

"No, but—"

"But what? I need release and I need it now. So do it."

She hadn't lost all her powers, she thought with satisfaction. The man began hastily undressing, a look of astonishment on his face as though he wasn't sure why his hands ripped off his clothes.

She pulled him down on top of her. When he lay on her body, a look of incredible hunger came over him and he plunged his cock straight inside her.

It always took them a few minutes, but they inevitably wanted her in the end. All except those damn twins, sons of Zeus—arrogant bastards.

She took out her anger on the man, making him take her in many ways, because she was so *hungry*. She'd fuck him until he was her slave and then he'd do anything for her, even die.

When she finally let him up, he was whimpering in exhaustion.

"I need clothes," she said. "I want to wander the world."

Shaking all over, the man drew on his own clothes and departed. She knew he wouldn't lock the door or run for help and he didn't.

She waited until he returned with a dress and some sandals, which she stared at in disbelief. "You want me to wear *these?*"

"I'm sorry, I—didn't know what to get."

He bowed his head, waiting for her to strike him. Selena put her hand on the back of his neck and scratched just deeply enough to draw blood.

"You can make it up to me," she said, smiling sweetly. "I need you to help me find a jar."

He blinked. "Jar?"

"Yes, two handles, had a picture of twins fucking a woman who looked just like me. I need to find out what happened to it."

The man looked blank and she slapped him across the face. "But first, we're going to find me some decent clothes."

She put on the dress then took him by the ear and marched him out the door.

The unused back room turned out to be attached to a small apartment with a few tiny chambers and a small kitchen. *A peasant*, she thought in disgust. She'd chosen a peasant to introduce her to the world again. Ah, well, he'd be fine until she could find something better.

The man led her out into streets that had changed in some ways but were the same in others. The vehicles and clothes and buildings were different, but the way people moved about, living their little lives hadn't changed. They didn't know anything, poor fools.

The peasant—Selena didn't bother asking what his name was because she didn't care—led her along the streets. People stared as they went by, and she held her head high, knowing they must all recognize that she was a demigoddess. She would restart her cult of worship soon.

She caught sight of her reflection in a shop window. The windows of this particular shop, rather than displaying wares, had black curtains cutting off the view of the interior, even though the shop was open.

The reflection showed herself, breasts nearly spilling out of the tight dress, legs long and strong, her sleek black hair flowing back to touch her ass. She smiled, liking what she saw.

But *shit*, she had to get new clothes.

"What is this shop?" she demanded.

The man swallowed, face pale. "An adult store."

"Aren't all stores for adults?"

"No, I mean where they sell, um…"

Selena solved the problem by striding to the door and shoving it open. "Ah, you mean sex toys. Excellent."

She dragged him inside. There she found exactly the clothes and shoes she needed and changed into them, watching in satisfaction while the man paid the bill. The black leather hugged her legs and pressed her breasts high. The black gloves fit perfectly, and the crowning touch was the whip.

It was a nice little whip which could be wound to a small coil, but she knew that its lash would sting.

Happy at last, she dragged her slave out of the store, back to his house, and spent the rest of the day playing with the whip and testing out her brand new black, spike-heeled shoes.

Next, she'd find the jar and the twins and take out her anger on them, and that would be that.

* * * * *

By two-thirty, when shops were beginning to close for the afternoon siesta, Fiona still had not found Cas and Pol. She'd searched the Plaka, the district of narrow, meandering streets around the high, flat-topped Acropolis, and found no trace of them.

She'd lost them in the flea market, and from there they could have gone any number of places. At one point she'd gotten it into her head that they'd probably gone back to the dig and she'd raced back, out of breath.

They hadn't been there. Hans Jorgensen, though, had discovered the loss of not only two pairs of jeans and a t-shirt, but his wallet as well. He was furious and frantic. Fiona slipped away again.

Down one of the narrow alleys on the other side of the flea market, she found a taverna overflowing with men singing and drinking wine. She peered into its dark depths but saw neither Cas nor Pol.

"Looking for someone, my angel?" a man at a sidewalk table asked her.

All his companions were men—in fact, there wasn't a woman in the place. Fiona blushed, remembering that Greek women usually wouldn't approach an all-male place, and foreign females who did could be mistaken for women on the make.

"Have you seen two men?" she asked in her best classroom Greek. "They are very tall and look alike. Twins."

All the men at the table nodded.

"Those two?" another man said. "Like the gods themselves came down for a cup of wine? They were here. Very generous."

Fiona hid a groan. "Did you see where they went?"

The men shrugged. A man at another table, younger than the others, gestured down the street, a cigarette stuck between his ring and middle fingers. "I saw them get into a taxi."

Fiona glanced at the corner as though Cas and Pol would conveniently materialize. "Damn," she muttered.

"It was Platonis' taxi," another man said. "He only takes tourists one place, and that's the Plataria, a taverna."

"They weren't tourists," the younger man argued. "They are Greek."

"But not from these parts."

The men shook their heads, murmuring agreement.

"Where is this Plataria place?" Fiona asked. When the men went stone-faced, uniting against a scolding woman, she said, "I need to find them. Please, it's important."

The younger man seemed to understand her distress. "It's in Omonia." He named a part of town that was a bit of a red light district. "Not for ladies. Wait at home, love. They'll come back."

Fiona choked back a frustrated snarl. She'd worked with academics and archaeologists so long she was not used to men who advised women to stay at home and leave their men alone.

Of course, these men couldn't know that she was chasing demigods from 500 B.C.E. who'd stolen her colleague's wallet and were busy enjoying themselves on Hans' credit cards.

As she hurried down the street, trying and failing to hail a cab, she wondered when she'd started believing they were truly demigods come to life. *Maybe that's the most convenient explanation*, she thought. *I should just report them to the police and go back to work.*

But as she frantically waved at taxis that wouldn't stop, she remembered the twins' warm weight on either side of her and the curious magic of their voices as they sang her to sleep the night before. The melody, so alien, had haunted her and given her dreams a brightness and incredible sensation, though they were blurry and half forgotten now.

Whoever the twins were, they weren't normal men. And they were out there in twenty-first century Athens with fifth century B.C.E. knowledge. She admitted it. She was worried about them.

* * * * *

Fiona would never have found them at all if it weren't for the music.

She at last persuaded a cab to stop for her and then used all her persuasion to get the driver to take her to Omonia, even though it was the beginning of the siesta time.

When she descended and paid the disapproving driver, the sun was hot overhead and doors and windows were closing against the heat of the day.

She had always approved of the siesta time, during which people rested out of the sun and started up again around six in the evening. It made sense to live in such a fashion in a warm climate, and the camaraderie she and her colleagues found in the coffee houses and tavernas at night more than made up for the inconvenience of closed shops in the middle of the day.

But this afternoon she ground her teeth as she walked past dark shops with locked doors, trying to find the taverna called the Plataria. The cab driver, like the men by the flea market, hadn't wanted to tell her exactly where it was.

She ducked into a tiny side alley to escape a motorist hurtling up the narrow street, and then she heard it.

Someone behind a window down the row was plucking a slow, sweet melody from a stringed instrument, and a warm, sensual baritone voice accompanied it. As the notes flowed over her, the music seemed to heat her skin, much like the sun that trickled into the alley.

45

She knew the voice. It was Cas, humming a song similar to the one he'd sung to her last night. He slid in words now and again, mostly about beautiful limbs and sweet honey on his tongue.

Slowly Fiona walked down the alley, drawn by the music, no longer frantic. The song soothed her, convincing her that all her worries were for nothing.

Come and listen, the melody whispered. *There is no hurt here.*

A blue painted door stood open, leading the way inside a dim taverna. The place was deserted, customers obviously gone home for siesta, except for Cas and Pol, sitting on painted wooden chairs before a cold fireplace, and a woman.

The woman was a belly dancer, replete with gauzy harem pants, tiny top and veils. She lay nearly flat on the floor, her legs folded under her while she leaned all the way back, her arms and hands moving sinuously. It was a position that must have taken much practice to master, and Fiona felt a twinge of envy and admiration.

The woman was likely Turkish, or descended from the Greeks made to leave the mainland of Turkey years ago. She had long black hair that blended with her veils and a lovely face painted with makeup.

Cas continued to sing. He leaned negligently in the chair, a cup of wine dangling from his hand, eyes languid. Next to him, Pol softly played a *laoúta*, a mandolin-like instrument, accompanying his brother and watching the woman.

The taverna hung with heat and a sensuality that tangled Fiona's senses and pulled her inside.

When the doorway darkened, Cas looked around, breaking off the heady music. He smiled, his gaze smoldering all the way across the room. "Fiona."

Pol also grinned at her, but he didn't stop playing. "Fiona, our goddess. Come in and dance."

What Fiona should have done was scold the pair of them, demand Hans' wallet and drag them back to the dig to make recompense.

What she did was lean against the doorframe, twining her hands together. "I don't know how to dance."

The woman rose from the floor with enviable grace. She held out her hands to Fiona but said nothing, likely not speaking English.

Cas gestured to the dancer with his wine cup. He truly looked like a god, lounging in the chair that emphasized his large body, his curled hair missing only its crown of leaves. He'd acquired a t-shirt somewhere — this one reading "Athens, City of Wonders" — but it didn't take away the divinity she sensed from him.

"She will teach you," Cas said. "Dance for us, Fiona."

The young woman smiled and came toward Fiona. She seemed to understand what Cas wanted and drew Fiona to the center of the room.

Pol played a little faster and Cas hummed along. The woman began snapping her fingers to the beat, which made Fiona think of harem tents and sheiks and men smoking hookahs.

Smiling at Fiona, the young woman moved her arm softly to the side, fingers bent, and nodded at Fiona to imitate her. Fiona held her arm awkwardly, knowing damn well she was not a dancer. The Turkish woman gently reached over and positioned Fiona's fingers correctly, middle finger pressed inward, as though she held an imaginary cymbal between finger and thumb.

The woman swayed her hips. It looked so easy, but Fiona's legs refused to move in the sensual swirl. She tried, then laughed at her own efforts.

Cas continued to hum. His eyes were dark, almost inky black, like the heavens with no stars. He did not laugh but watched Fiona in her knee-length shorts and loose blouse as though she were the sexiest creature alive.

The belly dancer showed Fiona simple arm movements, how to circle her wrists while lowering her arms in front of her, how to rotate her hips by swirling her ankles.

A smile creased Pol's face he watched Fiona try to master the moves. She didn't mind his teasing look—a gorgeous-as-sin man grinning at her didn't bother her in the least.

Pol increased the beat. Fiona shot him an exasperated look, and he laughed out loud. His laughter was beautiful, velvet and warm. Cas continued to hum, the throaty sound making Fiona warm all over.

Suddenly, she caught onto the moves the woman was trying to teach her. They danced together, legs and arms moving in unison.

Fiona was delighted. "I never knew belly dancing was so much fun."

Cas rose from his chair. Pol continued to play, and the woman continued her dance. The temperature in the room increased, Fiona sweating from the heat and her movements and the look on Cas' face as he crossed the room to her, still humming the unnerving melody.

He stood behind her, his tall body towering over hers. Fiona halted her dance as his strong, sun-bronzed arms slid around her waist from behind. His hips moved against hers, the zipper of his jeans pressing to the small of her back.

He gathered her to him and swayed in time to Pol's music. His hips rocked with sensuous grace, and he pulled her to sway with him, legs strong against her thighs.

Fiona closed her eyes. His broad chest pressed her back, his hands rested on the curve of her waist. Without thinking about what she was doing, she eased her hands onto his, feeling the sinews of his fingers. The heat of his body covered hers like a blanket.

The feel of his cock against the crease of her buttocks pooled warmth at the join of her legs. His breath in her ear as he leaned in to nibble it only stirred the fire.

The music went on. Cas continued the dance, his chest vibrating with the strange tune, his body seducing hers without him saying a word.

Fiona lost track of what the other woman did and where she was. Pol played on, the sound of the strings weaving through her mind, making her sleepy and wide awake at the same time.

Time slowed and moved like thick syrup on a winter day. Her senses narrowed to three—she heard the notes of the mandolin and Cas' song, she smelled the musk of Cas wrapping her body and she felt his tall form against her back.

When she opened her eyes, the shadows in the room had lengthened and the belly dancer had disappeared. Pol, his eyes dark with desire, set the *laoúta* aside and rose from his chair.

Instinctively, Fiona stepped back, but Cas was there holding her. Pol stopped before her, his scent tangling with Cas'. "You dance well, goddess."

He was as tall as Cas. The t-shirt stretched over his firm pectorals and shoulders, his arms corded with muscle.

Fiona had a hard time breathing. "What happened to the dancer?"

"She went home," Cas said.

"She had to get supper for her husband and daughter," Pol put in.

The explanation sounded so normal, so prosaic, that Fiona gasped with laughter. Then her laughter died when Pol lifted his hands and squeezed her nipples through her shirt.

At the same time, Cas unbuttoned the waistband of her shorts.

She gasped again. "What are you doing?"

"Giving you pleasure," Pol said.

Cas murmured in her ear, "The least we can do for rescuing us."

"But..." She cast a worried glance at the open door. "Someone could come in. Anyone could."

"Maybe they'd like to watch." Cas' breath scalded her ear and trickled heat down her spine. "Maybe I want them to watch me pleasuring you."

Fiona's knees started to bend. "No," she whispered.

Pol laughed. He gestured to the door with one hand and it swung closed.

The wind? Fiona thought wildly. But no breeze stirred the narrow passage outside or rattled the shutters.

"She's shy," Pol said, his fingers delicately pulling her nipples into hard little nubs.

Cas slowly lowered the zipper of Fiona's shorts, a loud zzzz in the stillness. "It took me a while to catch on to how these worked."

She remembered faintly why she had followed them and that she was supposed to be lecturing them. "You shouldn't have taken Hans' clothes. Or his wallet."

Pol flicked his thumbs over her hard-pointed nipples. "We will make recompense."

"Oh." She believed them. She had no idea why. But she relaxed, relieved. It would be all right.

That is, she relaxed until Cas slid strong fingers into her loosened shorts and pressed aside the elastic of her underwear.

Chapter Four

⥍

Cas' cock hardened at the sound of Fiona's groan. He smelled her female desire in the hot room and knew Pol did too.

The wiry hairs of her quim tickled his fingers. "You feel good, sweeting."

He wondered if her pussy looked as good as it felt. She was swimming with cream, the liquid all over his fingers.

"Make her come," Pol said. His brother continued to tease her nipples, his eyes intense and dark.

"Do you want to come, Fiona?" Cas asked, nibbling the shell of her ear. "We want to thank you for saving us."

"Thank you," Pol echoed.

Cas moved his fingers through her cream, easily slipping a finger into her opening. "Zeus above, but you're wet."

Pol smiled in delight.

Fiona whimpered. Her fire-red hair warmed his lips. He parted her opening and rubbed the folds of it. She nearly came, he felt it, her heartbeat speeding, her face gleaming in sudden perspiration.

"Someone might come in," she repeated.

"And what would they see?" Cas rested his head against hers, whispering into her hair. "They'd see my hand inside your clothes. They'd see Pol with his fingers on your breasts. They'd smell your desire and know you flowed like honey on my hands."

She made a gurgling noise. Pol took a step back and quickly popped open the button of his leggings and pulled down the metal fastening. He wore nothing beneath, and his cock spilled out, dark and hard.

"These leggings are too tight," he said. "I'm in pain."

"Jeans," Fiona said faintly.

"What?" Cas whispered.

"They're called jeans. Not leggings."

Cas chuckled. "I will remember. Pol is very hard for you. Do you want to touch him?"

Her cream flowed faster. "No."

"Your body just told me you did. Don't be afraid."

Pol moved closer to her, his hands on her waist, splaying his fingers under her breasts. "Touch me, my goddess. Bless me with your magic."

Fiona drew a breath as though she wanted to say something then she broke off. Tentatively, she reached her fingers toward Pol's rigid cock and laid them across the shaft.

"*Gods*," Pol breathed.

"That's it," Cas said. "Make him like it."

She moved her fingers to the tip while she leaned back into Cas. Cas enjoyed himself playing with her folds, then he dipped his first two fingers inside her, sinking them all the way. Fiona moaned and shifted her sweet backside provocatively on his cock, which was just as hard as Pol's.

"You feel like fire," Cas said as he leaned to nibble her neck. "You're squeezing my fingers so hard."

She arched back against him, unconsciously squeezing still more. To reward her, Cas slid in a third finger.

"Oh," she said, eyes wide.

Pol smiled. He stood with hands on hips, his body swaying as he felt what she did to him. "I think she likes it."

"Goddesses like to be pleasured." Cas bit her skin, loving the salt taste of it. "Don't they, my goddess?"

"I'm not a goddess. I'm an arch…" Her words faltered as Cas added a fourth finger. "…aeologist." The syllables tumbled out in a rush.

"You freed us," Pol whispered. "It was a terrible spell, and you freed us. Only a lady of great power could do that."

Fiona frowned as though she wanted to argue but her eyelids drooped. She pressed herself against Cas' hand, the yearning woman taking over the shy scholar. At the same time, she rubbed her palm over Pol's cock from tip to base and back again.

Cas would have envied him if her ass hadn't been rubbing all over him. He quickly unfastened his—*jeans*—releasing his cock to bump happily against the thin fabric across Fiona's backside.

She laid her head against his shoulder, her warm hair escaping its confinement to flow across his chest. She was so beautiful, her eyes so brown with gold flecks swimming in them, lashes long and lush against her cheek. A woman or a demigoddess or an archaeologist—whoever she was, she was made for loving.

Cas flicked his thumb over the hard nub of her clit. She jumped and squealed, coming back down to impale herself even farther on his fingers.

"Oh my God," she cried.

"Demigod," Cas murmured.

Pol was moaning softly, pushing his cock into her hand, his head thrown back, eyes closed.

Fiona squirmed against Cas' pressing fingers, her pussy so wet and slick he had to concentrate on keeping his hand inside her. He slid his thumb back and forth on the hard berry of her clit, stirring up even more cream.

She rose up on her toes, her heartbeat speeding, her breath coming in gasps. And then she came, beautifully and completely.

Her eyes flew open, her lips parting in astonishment. Her hips rocked faster and faster, seeking the pressure of Cas' fingers deep inside her and at the same time rubbing her clit hard against his thumb.

She clamped her hand down on Pol's cock, knuckles whitening as she clutched him. He moaned, shaking his hair back, and moved his hand over hers, helping her stroke while she squeezed.

The heady scent of her juices filled Cas' senses. He made a quiet noise as she continued to come, her breath hot on his face, her cries of pleasure in his ear.

Pol came all at once, putting his hand over his sweating face, swallowing groans. Fiona rose on her tiptoes, stroking Pol's cock, rubbing her ass against Cas and pressing herself down onto his hand.

Cas sank his teeth into her neck, enjoying the taste of her skin, the salt of her perspiration. "That's it, love," he murmured, licking where he'd bitten.

They moved together a little longer, all three of them in pleasure, Fiona and Pol mindless with it, Cas smiling and watching and feeling Fiona.

Fiona lost her hold on Pol's cock. Pol backed away, throwing his head back and dragging in deep breaths, trying to calm down. Fiona closed her eyes and bumped and danced against Cas.

He pinched her clit and she screamed once, then drifted down into babbling incoherencies.

"Sweet Fiona," he breathed into her ear.

Then all three of them began to calm, the shattering moment unwinding into warm stillness. Outside the window, people shuffled through the alley, the city waking again from its afternoon nap.

Fiona opened her eyes. She looked back at Cas, eyes languid, then at Pol, who'd sat down on the wooden chair, face in his hands, his cock still out and gleaming. She stared at Pol then at Cas again.

She realized what she'd just done and blushed furiously.

"She's shy," Cas said, laughter welling up inside him. "How adorable."

"I like her," Pol said.

"So do I." Cas leaned down and kissed her, a slow decadent kiss that told her he'd stamped her as his own.

When he released her, she'd scarcely a moment to draw a breath before Pol, who'd risen from the chair again, tilted her head back and claimed his own kiss.

Two demigods, one on either side of her, identical twins. This had to be paradise.

"Our own goddess," Cas murmured. "What could be better?"

* * * * *

"I keep trying to explain I am *not* a goddess." Fiona sat between Pol and Cas in an eatery that was dark but lively with patrons, blood-red wine and excellent food.

Cas lifted his glass to his lips. She couldn't help focusing on him as he tipped wine into his mouth, swallowed slowly, and chased a red drop from his lip with his tongue. "Goddess, sorceress, archaeologist, whatever you call yourself, it was powerful magic that freed us."

After a brief cleanup in a tiny bathroom at the taverna, Cas and Pol announced they were hungry and it was high time to eat. They wandered out of the alley and to another pedestrian area with sidewalk cafés and shops stretching the length of the street.

They'd ducked arbitrarily into a café's interior and the waiter brought them a jug of wine and three glasses. Without bothering to look at the menu, Pol and Cas ordered a full roast with whatever fruits they had and bread, as fresh as could be had.

The waiter stared at them then turned around and bellowed to the kitchen. A responding bellow came that fine, they'd do whatever Cas and Pol wanted.

The pair didn't seem to have any trouble getting people to fulfill their every desire. They'd usurped the best table in the café, and now the cook was happy to make a special feast just for them.

And they'd convinced Fiona not only to *not* yell at them about taking off to the taverna and stealing from Hans, she'd let the two of them pleasure her. *Together.*

It had been a long time since Fiona's last sexual encounter. She'd broken up with her previous boyfriend three years ago, in grad school for heaven's sake. And never in the eighteen-month relationship with him had she felt what the twins had made her feel in the empty taverna.

No sex for three years, and then bam, she had a pleasure session with *two men at the same time*. When had life gotten so out of hand?

But Cas stroking her had made her nearly explode with passion. Not to mention holding Pol's warm shaft in her hand, letting his tip bump her palm with satin softness and the slick heat of his come slide over her fingers.

Never in her wildest, wildest dreams would she have thought she'd be pleasured by two identical, gorgeous hunks of men at the same time.

Hunks of men who thought she was a goddess or at least some sort of magical being.

"All I did," she repeated, "was find the pieces of the jar and put it back together."

"And how did you find all the pieces?" Cas asked. "How did you know to put them together?"

His hand slid to her thigh, touching the skin bared by her shorts. She cleared her throat.

"By working my butt off. I surveyed and took notes and hunted and sorted through thousands of pieces of pottery before I found the right ones. The vessel must have been shattered in one place and the pieces moved. Usually pots are found on a garbage dump or shoved to the corner of a room. The pieces might be scattered, but not that much. Pieces of this one turned up in a huge variety of places, as though they had been deliberately separated."

"I'm not surprised," Pol said grimly. "You say you are not magic, but why should you repair the vessel unless you knew to break the spell?"

"Curiosity." She bit her lip, thinking. "No, I admit I was drawn to it. When I had enough together to see that it had the portrait of a beautiful man on it, I wanted to keep going. It was a biceps that came together first."

She glanced at Cas', which were brawny and strong without being too huge.

"I wonder whose," Pol said, eyes twinkling. "His or mine."

"I don't know." Her face heated. "Everyone calls it 'Fiona's sex jar', because the painting is so erotic. What was it meant to be?"

Pol lost his smile. "A spell."

"A trap," Cas added. "By a demon demigoddess whose anger surpassed her reason." The muscles of his jaw hardened, his eyes dark with old rage. "She tried to murder Pol."

Pol gestured with his wine cup. "She used me as bait so Cas would come running to save my life. As soon as we were together, she started weaving the spell, trapping us in the painting."

"Why?" Fiona asked. "Why should she want you in a painting?"

She glanced at both twins, taking in their attractive physiques, molten dark eyes and handsome-as-sin faces. She supposed that in a painting, a person could look at them whenever they wished—but not to be able to touch them or hear them or taste them? What was the demigoddess thinking?

Not to mention caging them up for several thousands of years. That was just wrong.

Cas set his wine glass on the table and smoothed a lock of Fiona's unruly hair. "The idea was that we'd be trapped copulating with her for eternity. I don't think it worked, because there was—nothing."

"That's evil," Fiona said indignantly. "Why should she do such a thing? I mean, I understand why a woman would want to have sex with you—believe me, I do—but that seems a little extreme."

Pol sloshed more wine into his cup then Fiona's. "Ah, but she was a woman scorned. Scorned by us."

"She wanted us," Cas said bluntly. "And we said no."

Fiona studied him, curious. "Why did you say no? Well all right, apart from her being an evil demigoddess and trying to kill Pol."

"Just because we have healthy sexual appetites," Pol said, "doesn't mean we drop our clothes for every women who walks by. She wanted us to pledge ourselves to her and champion her and help her move up the goddess hierarchy. She more or less wanted us to be her slaves and couldn't understand when we objected."

"So she decided we'd be with her for eternity," Cas said. "She bound us with very strong magic and forced us to perform the sexual ritual, and then—oblivion."

Fiona shivered. "I'm so sorry."

"Which you released us from." Pol raised her hand to his lips. The touch of his sensual mouth on her skin started the fires between her legs again, not that they'd really damped down. "With your magic called *archaeology*."

Cas turned his wine glass moodily. "The problem is, if we are free, I imagine she is free as well."

"Her image disappeared from the vessel," Fiona said. "Yours didn't. Maybe that means you got free and she didn't."

"I do not want to count on this," Cas answered. "She might be out there right now, in Athens, searching for you, wanting her vengeance for freeing us."

Fiona stared at him. "But she was trapped in oblivion too. Wouldn't she be out celebrating that she's free? The spell obviously went wrong. Why should she be angry at me for that?" She looked at both their faces. Cas was frowning, and Pol still looked grim. "Oh, I forgot, she's an evil demigoddess."

"She never liked to be thwarted," Pol said. "She won't like it now."

"I always thought of gods and goddesses as good," Fiona said. "Well, within reason. They fight amongst themselves but aren't too bad toward normal humans. Demigod means half human, half god. What is this demigoddess's name, and which of the Pantheon was her father?"

"She called herself Selena," Pol said. "She was spawned by Poseidon and a she-demon of great power."

"Oh," Fiona said. "That can't be good."

Cas drew his finger across her cheek, the warmth tingling her skin. "No. As you say, that can't be good."

She kissed his finger, feeling daring. "I'll do what I can to help," she said.

Cas smiled his slow, heated smile that made her remember his fingers penetrating her, bringing her to pleasure with intense, wild friction. "We know. That's why we like you."

Pol lifted her hand to his lips. "And why we'll give you all the pleasure you want in return."

"All the pleasure?" she asked faintly.

"Anything you want," Cas said, nuzzling her. "What do you want, Fiona?"

She wanted *them*.

Good lord, what was the matter with her? She'd never wanted unconventional sex in her life. Never dreamed she ever would have it.

And now she wanted more of it. Someone needed to hose her down, because she was burning up.

Cas and Pol watched her intently, waiting for her answer, their dark eyes pools of wanting.

Fiona swallowed hard. "Look," she babbled, relieved. "Here comes the food."

* * * * *

The twins' worry about the demon demigoddess did not make them rush back to the dig to find answers and hide from her. Instead, they settled down to enjoy the extensive meal brought lovingly by the waiters.

Fiona ate sparingly, enjoying the food but too stunned by the events of the day and the night before to be able to concentrate on eating. The twins, on the other hand, ate everything, passing compliment after compliment to the cooks.

They had meat and wine and fruit and more wine and cheese and more wine and sweet sticky baklava and more wine. They remained at the restaurant for three hours, talking and eating and laughing with Fiona and total strangers.

Just when Fiona was wondering how they were going to pay for all of it and whether she would have to foot the bill, Cas held up a plastic card and handed it to the waiter.

Fiona spluttered, coughing up wine. Pol thumped her on the back as the waiter disappeared into the back with the card.

"That's Hans Jorgensen's credit card. You can't use that."

"On the contrary, Fiona, everyone wishes me to pay with this card."

"But you stole it from him—when you stole his clothes, I might add."

"Borrowed," Pol corrected. "We will acquire our own and return them. He was the only man we saw who was the same size and shape we are."

"He won't be so understanding when he reports you to the police for stealing his credit card and going on a spending spree."

"But we are spending nothing," Cas said. "We give the card and all is given to us. Everyone in Athens will soon know that Hans Jorgensen likes their wares and their food. I am writing his name so *he* will be thanked, not me."

Pol nodded, his face flushed with wine. "'Tis generous of you, brother."

"Oh, gods."

Fiona laid her head on the cool wooden table. How on earth was she to explain credit cards to demigods who hadn't gone out in twenty-five hundred years? Athenians had been sophisticated when it came to money, but she wasn't quite sure what a modern equivalent would be.

She raised her head and heaved a sigh. "They aren't giving you the things because you have a card. I mean, they are but..." She started again. "It's like a running tally. The card keeps track of everything that's spent and at the end of the month, Hans receives one really — big — bill."

Both Pol and Cas frowned over this. Then Cas said, "You mean we are buying on credit."

"Yes," she said, relieved. "That's what I mean."

"You should have said so." The waiter put the bill down in front of Cas and he lifted the pen and wrote *Hans Jorgensen* in a practiced manner. Fiona bit back a groan.

"Don't worry, Fiona," Cas said, smiling his sinful smile. "We will pay him."

"How?" She lowered her voice. "You don't have any money."

Pol exchanged a knowing look with Cas. "But we know where some is. And Hans will get it all."

Somehow, this didn't make Fiona feel any better.

They left the restaurant. It was well dark now, and Fiona assumed they'd return to the dorm. But as soon as they left the café, Pol lifted his head and said, "I hear music."

Most of the cafés and tavernas featured singing and dancing that lasted well into the night and early morning. The street was crowded with people walking or standing in groups talking to the people who sat in tables at the outdoor cafés.

Cas slid his arms around Fiona's waist as Pol strode off in search of whatever music had caught his attention. They strolled along behind, keeping Pol's tall form in view.

"I want you." Cas' lips touched her ear, his voice low and sensuous.

She gave a shaky laugh. "Demigods aren't much for being subtle are they?"

"I mean I want you for myself. Just me." His breath tickled deep inside her, lighting fires all the way.

The heat made her blush. "So you and Pol usually…"

"Share. Yes." His fingers slid to the small of her back. "But this time I think I want you to myself. Mine to savor. Alone."

She had the sudden vision of herself and Cas standing in a warm room, her dorm room, for instance, their clothes on the floor, their hands all over each other. She thought about the way she'd held Pol's huge cock in her hands, but it had been Cas who'd stroked her, held her, and demanded nothing from her.

"What about Pol?" she asked as tingling invaded her entire body.

"Pol is rarely left without companionship. Women love him. He is, I think the English word is *outgoing*, always with laughter and jests on his lips. He is irresistible, I am told. While I am perhaps not as interesting."

64

"Don't think that." Fiona stopped. "You're more thoughtful and quiet but plenty interesting. Trust me."

He gave her a half smile and smoothed a ringlet on her forehead. "I wish you for myself, Fiona Archaeologist."

"McCarty. My last name is McCarty. Archaeology is what I do."

"It is a part of you," Cas said. "It is what you are, this archaeology, this magic that made you search for pieces of a pot scattered across these islands. I want to explore that part of you, Fiona."

He brushed his lips to the corner of her mouth, sending fires dancing through her.

"I imagine you want to explore other parts of me too," Fiona smiled into his skin.

Cas grinned, his eyes suddenly lighting. "All of you, my goddess."

Chapter Five

✍

They found Pol in a taverna already dancing to the sounds of a stringed *laoúta*, his arms over his head, his feet tracing complicated patterns on the floor. Cas procured himself and Fiona a table near the center of the taverna, and they sat down to watch Pol.

Pol danced well for a man so tall and muscular. He moved with a sinuous grace that was all masculine and every female in the place appreciated it. He snapped his fingers with the beat and the drinkers at the tables around him clapped or snapped fingers with him.

He moved his feet as languidly as had the belly-dancer, his hands making sharper gestures than hers. His black hair glistened in the candlelight, his swarthy face gleaming with perspiration.

"He loves attention," Cas said, sounding amused. He'd pulled his seat close to Fiona's and draped his arm across the back of her chair.

Another man joined Pol on the floor, one with white hair and an obvious experience with dancing. He danced slowly around Pol, the two men moving in harmony. After a time, another man joined with his wife.

Fiona looked up at Cas to find his face close to hers, his eyes holding a fire that could have burned down the taverna. She wondered where her shyness had gone. Two days ago, she would have writhed with embarrassment to be this close to a man, especially when it was obvious what he had in mind.

Now she gazed back at him, her heartbeat quick, then raised her face to his and met his lips in a kiss.

His warm mouth brushed hers and he kissed the corner of her lips, darting his tongue briefly over her skin. Her female places went molten—she swore there was lava down there.

She kissed him again, following his lead to take it slowly. His eyes closed, thick black lashes resting on his bronzed cheeks. He nuzzled her, then kissed her upper lip. She caught his lower between hers and sucked.

Cas made a noise of satisfaction. He drew back, eyes half-closed, the gleam from beneath his lids wicked.

On the floor, Pol continued to dance. He had his gaze on the dancing woman, a fact which the woman noticed and her husband did not. Pol winked and she blushed.

"I see my brother might be keeping himself busy tonight," Cas murmured. He slid his arm around Fiona's shoulders and eased her gently back against him.

"But she's married," Fiona hissed.

Remembering stories of gods and demigods of the Greek Pantheon, she realized that none of them paid much attention to the marital status of the person they wanted. The only reason Zeus had disguised himself as animals or rain or whatever was because he didn't want his wife Hera to know he was off philandering. He hadn't been particular about whether the woman of his affections was married or single.

"Few women can resist Pol," Cas said.

Fiona flushed. "Including me, it seems. I've never done that before. You know, with two."

"There's a first time for everything." He cuddled her close and pressed a warm kiss to her hair. "I hope the second time is with me."

"Will Pol mind?"

What is wrong with me? I'm asking a man if his brother minds if he doesn't do a ménage a trois with us.

"He knows how to keep himself busy."

Cas skimmed his thumb along Fiona's jaw and turned her face to his. This kiss was still slow, but fuller, his mouth slanting all the way across hers. Her blood ran hot, sweat prickling on her forehead, and the cream between her thighs was definitely lavalike.

He dipped his tongue into her mouth gently but completely and delved expertly to taste every corner of her.

When she came up for air, she saw Pol staring at them. His look was not possessive like Cas', but almost feral. He seemed to like watching his brother kiss Fiona so thoroughly.

"Let us walk," Cas said. He scraped his chair back and rose, his large body dwarfing hers as he waited, his hand on her chair.

"What about Pol?"

Cas slid his gaze to his brother who was dancing again. The beat had increased and Pol's steps became faster and more intricate. Someone whooped.

"He'll be fine. He likes to show off."

"But he doesn't know how to get back to the dorm. Should we leave him?"

"We will not go far."

Hand on the small of her back, Cas steered Fiona through the maze of tables and chairs and out into the cool night. The street was still lively, the sidewalks filled with people lounging and drinking and smoking, music spilling out of doors.

Fiona liked Athens best at this time of night. The work day was over, the night air refreshing, and everyone relaxed and chatted under the streetlights and the stars.

"It was like this in the Athens of old," Cas said. "Except the married women stayed inside. I like to see the women outside, walking freely."

Fiona grinned. "An ancient Athenian feminist."

"I have not heard this word *feminist*. But why should women be locked away like prisoners? Men should be allowed to look even if they cannot touch."

Fiona tucked her arm through his. "Well, I don't think your motives are exactly pure, but I sure wouldn't want to be confined to my home. But then, when I said I wanted to be an archeologist, people wondered why I didn't want to get married instead. Not that it was a difficult choice, because no one asked me to marry them."

"I am glad they did not. I would have to fight them or trick them to get to you, because I am determined to have you."

Her heart did a little flutter. "You're very sweet."

His look told her he didn't know what she was talking about. She decided to say nothing more and just enjoy walking next to a tall, delicious man with beautiful black eyes who wanted to be with her.

"When did you begin to believe me?" Cas asked. They reached the end of the street and turned into a narrower lane, replete with shadows.

"Hmm?"

"When we first appeared in your bed, you did not believe we were demigods from your vessel. Why do you now?"

She thought a moment, twining her fingers more firmly around his forearm.

"I don't know, really. I figured if you want to say you're demigods from 500 B.C.E., why shouldn't I let you? Either you're telling the truth and believing you is the least I can do, or you're making it up as a joke, in which case, who am I to stand in the way of your fun?"

He slanted a smile at her that was full of promise. "It sounds very logical."

"Yes, it does to me too. I think. Why are we here?"

Cas had led her around another corner into a sheltered walkway between streets. It had been turned into a strip of hidden garden with a latticed roof laced with vines and roses, a gravel walkway, more vines on the walls, high where they could reach the sun, and wooden benches.

"Why do you think?" he said, then he kissed her, a full-blown assault this time.

His tongue reached deep into her mouth, possessing it, telling her firmly, *You are mine.* He tasted incredibly sweet, the rich dark wine he'd drunk mellow and soft on her tongue. She twined her arms around his neck, liking having someone want her so much.

The kiss was hard and demanding, his mouth opening hers, lips bruising. Fiona had never really believed women sighed in surrender—it was only what she read in romance novels—but her knees weakened and she let out a moan that was pure surrender. She'd wave a white flag if she had one.

"Fiona," he whispered as he moved his mouth to her cheek, her forehead, her chin. His shoulders bunched as he kissed her throat, his kisses including little licks that sent shock waves through her body.

"What if someone comes?" Her voice was weak, as though she couldn't think why she was protesting at all.

"What if they do?" He smiled, breath hot on her face. "What if they see you, beautiful Fiona, and me loving you?" He slid his hand into her blouse and began to undo buttons.

"No, really, it's a public walkway."

He led her a few feet down the path to the shadows next to a bench. "Better?"

"No."

"Let them watch." He kissed her parted lips, darted his tongue inside, then evaded her when she tried to kiss him back. "Do you like being watched?"

"No. I don't know. I never have been."

He pried open more buttons, working his way down her shirt. Cool air touched her breasts which swelled over her sensible white bra. He touched the top seam, fingertip brushing her skin. "I want this off. How does it work?"

"In the back."

She reached behind herself but Cas slid his hand inside her shirt and began to work at the clasps.

A demigod from ancient Greece shouldn't know how to undo bra hooks, she thought, and he didn't. He played with them for a long time before they finally burst free.

"Did your other lovers never display you?" Cas asked as he eased her shirt and bra from her shoulders. Both garments hung from her lower arms, and she froze, her breasts exposed to outside air for the first time in her life. "Did they never show others how beautiful you were?"

Stunned surprise chased shock then amusement through her brain. "Hardly. Charles, my boyfriend in grad school, didn't even want to display me to himself. He always kept the light off."

"Perhaps *he* had something to hide," Cas suggested. "There is no reason to conceal this beauty."

He traced his fingers over the sides of her breasts then to her areolas, which were already hard and tight for him.

"You think I'm beautiful?" Could she sound any more wistful?

"What I *think* does not matter. Your beauty is a fact."

She shivered hard, so wanting to believe him. No one had ever called Fiona McCarty, Ph.D., dusty archaeology postdoc, beautiful.

"I think you're flattering me so you can get into my pants," she said, then she blushed, remembering the taverna and Cas pressed behind her. "No wait, you already got into my pants."

"Every moment of this afternoon was unforgettable. I want more."

"You make me want you too."

"Good." He drew out the word, breathing into her hair.

"I don't trust myself," she whispered as she slid her hands around his neck.

"Then trust me."

She closed her eyes, already knowing she wasn't going to fight. *Don't lose your heart, Fiona*, she chided herself. *He showed up out of nowhere and he'll take what he wants and disappear back to nowhere, leaving you in the dust. It's what happens with gorgeous men like him.*

Yes, but gorgeous men like him never happen to me.

She had no intentions of pushing him away. She kissed him as he went back to swirling his fingers around her areolas. If he was going to leave her in the dust, why shouldn't she enjoy the heck out of him first? She'd go in with no expectations. Expectations were what got you hurt.

No way could she push him away anyway. Her entire body was on fire, cream ran rampant between her legs and he was so strong.

Cas sat on the bench and pulled her to stand between his thighs. This made it easier for him to tilt his head and close his lips over her nipple. Fiona groaned and let her head drop back, thrusting herself farther into his mouth.

He suckled her, a sensation of both pleasure and pain. Her old boyfriend had occasionally played with her nipples while they had sex, but with Charles it had been pinch, pinch, thrust, thrust, *done,* and her lying there wondering what had happened.

Cas took his sweet time. He gave all his attention to her breast with lips and tongue and teeth and fingers, until her body heated to unbearable temperatures. As if sensing she was pushing the limit, Cas released her. Just as she drew a breath of mixed disappointment and relief, he switched to her left breast.

She murmured something incomprehensible even to herself and swirled her fingers through his black hair. She loved the feel of it, thick and silky, rampant with curls.

He moved his tongue around her left nipple, playing until it stood up as much as the right. Then he switched back and forth, sucking one, nipping the other, flicking his tongue over the first one, rubbing fingers gently over the second.

He was doing a good job driving her crazy. She rocked on the balls of her feet, her thighs wet and scalding with cream, *wanting* him. "Please, Cas."

"I'll let you release in a moment. Not yet."

"Why not?" she whimpered.

"I have not finished. I'll help you release when I'm ready."

"Please, please, please," she begged.

"When I am ready."

He went back to pleasuring her breasts. Her shirt sagged open, and he drew his tongue, a streak of fire, down to massage her navel. He went lower, as far as he could before running into her shirt and the waistband of her shorts.

He put his fingers under the waistband and slid the button through the hole. Fiona shivered in excitement, wishing he'd go on and thrust his fingers inside her like he had this afternoon.

She remembered the heat of his body behind her and his fingers moving through her slick opening, fucking her with his hand while she held onto the incredible heat of Pol's cock. It had been the loveliest experience of her life.

To her disappointment, Cas stopped at unbuttoning the waistband and sat back away from her. Before she could voice her sorrow, he grabbed the hem of his own shirt and pulled it off over his head.

She closed her mouth on her words and simply admired the moonlight on Cas. His torso, as she'd noted the night before, had sharply defined muscles, a shadowed hollow between the pectorals, and hard shoulders. Hair curled over his chest, black and wiry, his male nipples in perfect proportion. Dreamily, Fiona touched one nipple, happy to see it draw to a peak as tight as hers did.

"Do you like that?" she asked, a bit surprised.

"Do you?"

"Yes."

"That is your answer." He stood up and draped his shirt over the backless wooden bench. "Lie down."

This was getting out of hand. They were both half-undressed and this was still a public place.

But did she button up her shirt, tell him no and sensibly walk away? Of course not. She obediently plopped to the bench and swung her legs up to lie full length on it.

Cas unzipped her shorts and tugged them and underwear down her legs, releasing her right leg from them so that the fabric bunched around her left ankle. He pressed her thighs apart, making her straddle the bench.

"Perfect," he said, then he positioned himself between her thighs and kissed her quim.

No man had *ever* done that. A few men had wanted to, but Fiona had always felt shy about letting them see her private places, not sure she'd like it and fearing they wouldn't.

Cas didn't bother asking. He kissed her clit then worked kisses down to her opening, breath hot on her folds, whiskers abrading the soft flesh of her thighs. She squirmed and arched, begging with her body for him to do more and more.

The shirt beneath her softened the bench, containing warmth from his skin and Cas' heady scent.

Cas licked her, his tongue masterful. Her excitement spiraled and built, and suddenly she came, moaning into the night.

She pressed her hand over her mouth to stifle her cries, and Cas continued to torture her. He licked and played, delving his tongue deeper as she arched into him, and she prayed her noise wouldn't cause someone to hear and investigate. How embarrassing to have to explain an arrest for indecent exposure to Dr. Wheelan.

Cas raised his head and smiled at her, holding her down with both hands. "The torment of Aphrodite," he said. "She made sure that women would have the greatest of all pleasures." He touched the spot that in Latin was called the *mons Venus* — Aphrodite was Venus in the Greek.

Aphrodite had done her job. Fiona gasped and groaned, tears leaking from her eyes.

Cas at last withdrew his fingers, but the fever still hummed through her body. She felt happy and strong and ready for sex.

Instead of continuing to the next step, Cas lifted her and settled her in his lap. She tilted her head back to kiss him and the kiss went on, long and deep and taking.

She heard gravel crunch suddenly on the path. She gasped and broke the kiss. "Someone *was* watching."

Cas smoothed his hand through her hair. Her shirt sagged and her shorts were still wrapped around one leg, her breasts and quim exposed to the air.

"What if they were?" Cas whispered. "You are beautiful and gave them a lovely show."

"Terrific. Just what I always dreamed of."

"You should not be ashamed." His lips grazed her temple, breath burning. "Being watched turns me on in a big way. So does watching."

"It does?"

"Watching a woman pleasure herself is a heady thing. You learn exactly what she likes and exactly what brings her to ecstasy."

Fiona shivered, imagining his intense black gaze riveted to her while she dipped her fingers into her own quim. "Oh my," she said.

"Do it now."

Fiona turned to stare at him. He wore a smile on his lips, but his eyes held raw need.

"Now?"

He pushed her gently from his lap, and she landed shakily on her feet. "Now. Touch yourself for me, Fiona. I will warn you if anyone comes."

She didn't quite believe him, and she wondered if she *had* heard someone on the path before. It might have been a bird or animal, and in spite of the dark excitement flowing through her, she hoped so.

Cas wanted her to touch herself while he sat on the bench and watched. Dear gods. He expected it. He folded his arms across his chest, muscles playing, a slight breeze ruffling his hair as he waited.

Boldly, Fiona kicked off her shorts and set them on the bench. Her shirt and bra still hung from her arms but she left them there. The feel of the cotton loose against her skin aroused her, making her feel naughty.

She stuck her forefinger into her mouth and drew it out slowly, then she did what she'd never done in her life— probed her fingertip through her own folds.

She was wet and hot and her quim was tight. She'd never known. She'd lived with her femaleness all her life but she'd never explored or appreciated it.

Cas' raw, hot gaze helped her juices flow faster, wetting her fingers with scalding liquid. She'd come in her underwear before, but she'd never felt the honey with her hands, never touched the hard nub that released all her fantasies.

The pictures in her mind when she touched herself were incredible. First was Cas as he was, watching her. Next was herself kneeling before him, sucking him into her mouth with enthusiasm. Then she thought of him behind her on his knees, easing that huge cock into her while she screamed and writhed.

She put Pol in the shadows, watching with the same intense gaze Cas had now. And then she had Pol kneel in front of her, his cock heavy and long, bumping her lips until she pulled him into her mouth.

The last picture made her moan with longing. She pressed her hands hard against herself, legs parted, cream all over her fingers. She loved it, loved it, loved it.

Cas rose and came to her. He swiftly pulled her against him, his body almost assaulting her. He let her rub her wet quim over his jeans, making her orgasm go on and on.

Hot and sweet and rough, oh gods, I love this.

Cas' hands covered her buttocks as she writhed against his thick thigh. His mouth came down hard on hers, his tongue all over the place inside her as he caught her cries.

"Cas," she said, her voice ragged. "Do you want to—go all the way?"

"All the way? You mean fuck?"

"Yes. Yes, that's what I mean."

To her surprise and embarrassment, he shook his head. "Not yet, my love. Not because I don't want you, but because you must be ready."

"But…" She gulped for air. "I just let you lick me, and then I took off my shorts and played with myself for you—in a public garden."

"I know. And it was beautiful."

"I think it means I'm ready."

"Not yet." He held her hard, the hot friction of his jeans almost as satisfying as his tongue. She rocked a few more times, enjoying the fire.

"You like this?" he asked.

"Yes."

She continued to pleasure herself on him, amazed at herself. It felt so good to move against his powerful muscles, hearing him grunt softy as he held her with hard fingers.

"You are beautiful, Fiona."

She was coming again, but the only thing that would satisfy her, deeply satisfy her, was having him inside her. She remembered the pressure of his fingers in her quim and the feeling of his long cock pressed against her ass.

Fiona wanted that cock deep inside her and she wanted it *now*.

But he wouldn't give it to her now. She had the feeling that no matter how much she begged, he would have sex with her only when he decided it was time.

She wished it would be time quickly.

As her orgasm died away into little gasps, Cas lifted her in his arms then sat down on the bench and arranged her in his lap.

"You are the sweetest woman," he whispered against her hair. "You taste sweet and watching you come is delectable."

"I want to taste *you*." She touched his jaw and kissed his lips.

Cas laughed softly and gently lifted her shirt and bra over her shoulders again.

"I am forever grateful to you, Fiona. You have lessened the sadness of leaving behind all I knew. I missed so much, but now I have you." He returned her kiss with a deep one of his own, then he pushed her to her feet. "I have much to teach you, but later."

Fiona found herself standing in front of him bare-assed, shirt unbuttoned, scrutinized by his appreciative gaze. Her entire body was crying out for sex, and he knew it, if the smile on his face was anything to go by.

She took up her shorts and underwear from the bench. "When?" She hoped she didn't sound too eager and horny and needy and pathetic.

He lifted his shirt and pulled it on over his head. "We will have other opportunities for play." His smile turned dark. "I promise you. Now let us return to find Pol."

"Pol?" She started. "I thought you wanted me all to yourself."

He chuckled and gave her another searing kiss. "I do. But I am thirsty, and where we find wine, we will also find Pol."

He graciously gave her time to put on and zip up her shorts, then he slid his arm firmly around her shoulders and led her back out into Athens.

Chapter Six

ℬ

When they reached the archaeological compound again that night, Fiona found the twins an empty bedroom and told them they had to sleep there.

Pol gave her a glance filled with sin. "But we want to sleep with you, goddess. You saved us, and we are devoted to you."

"Yes, but if anyone finds out we shared a single bed, I'll lose my job. Postdocs to the Athenian Agora aren't handed out to just anyone, and I work my butt off for it."

Both twins turned their gazes to her backside, looking appreciative.

"I think it is still there," Pol said.

Cas nodded. "In the best possible way."

Fiona gurgled in frustration, threw blankets and pillows at them, and stalked from the room.

Back in her own bedroom, she got into her nightshirt and lay down, but sleep eluded her. Today had been one hell of a day. She'd spent half of it chasing two on-the-loose demigods, then having her first ménage as she stroked Pol and Cas brought her readily to orgasm.

Then all that food and drink and watching Pol dance, then Cas stealing off with her to the dark garden walk and having her stand in front of him and play with herself for him.

She shivered again, remembering the night air touching her exposed skin and her own hands working herself to orgasm. She'd never thought herself capable of it.

Pol and Cas were busily teaching her all that she was capable of.

At least Pol had been amenable to taking a taxi straight back to the dorm without suggesting they drive up to the Acropolis or something for more impromptu sex. Not that she didn't think it was coming.

She also reviewed their story of the demigoddess who'd ensorcelled them onto the jar. She'd never heard this about the legend of Castor and Pollux, the twins of the constellation Gemini, though she admitted she didn't know much about them.

She knew the story went that Castor and Pollux were very close brothers, and when Castor was slain—because the twins had carried off two women they wanted and then had to fight the ladies' suitors...typical of them—Pollux grieved so much that when Zeus made Pollux immortal, he asked if he could share the immortality with Cas.

Each day, one of the twins would reside in Hades, one in the heavens. Zeus eventually rewarded their loyalty to each other and made them both immortal. They were the brightest stars of the Gemini constellation and said to be lucky for sailing and good weather.

But the ancient Greeks had come up with many beautiful stories to explain phenomena such as constellations and odd rock formations and echoes and laurel trees. How much was true and how much imagination was difficult to know.

Perhaps the story had been made up to explain the constellation, while the real Cas and Pol lived on, getting themselves into and out of trouble. Then one day they'd met a lust-ridden demigoddess who wouldn't take no for an answer.

She ground her teeth. *Bitch.*

Fiona McCarty didn't say such words, but there was no other name for a woman who'd punish the twins because they wouldn't do the dirty with her. Sometimes people hit it off and sex was great, and sometimes it didn't happen. Most people faced rejection by walking away, licking their wounds, and finding someone else. But this woman had chosen to punish them by trapping them in oblivion for twenty-five hundred years.

Why oblivion? Fiona suddenly wondered. The demigoddess had meant to trap them into an eternal erotic game. After Fiona's own taste of the twins' sexuality today, she couldn't really blame the demigoddess for wanting to spend eternity enjoying sex with them, even though she would not have chosen such a cruel method.

But the demigoddess's trap hadn't worked. What had gone wrong?

Fiona got herself out of bed, pulled on her jeans under the nightshirt, thrust her feet into grubby sneakers, and padded out of her room. Outside the night was quiet, the area around the dorm a silent darkness.

Once upon a time the Agora had been the heart of the city, as bustling and thriving as the rest of Athens today. The Agora had housed the offices of government, temples to Apollo, Zeus, and other gods, and a huge marketplace. The *stoa* around the square had solid back walls and pillared walkways that invited people to step into the shade out of the hot sun.

All of Athens met here, the councils, the law courts and juries, merchants with goods from all corners of the known globe, the famous philosophers and the priests of the temples. It bustled with activity, color and life, much like the flea market and other pedestrian area markets of the city today.

Now it was dark and silent, its inhabitants long gone, with only the loving care of people interested in its rich past to remind people of the greatness that had gone before. The American School of Classical Studies had worked on this site for nearly a century, restoring and studying the heart of the ancient Athenian empire.

Fiona's specialty was pottery, so she pored over tiny fragments the archaeologists unearthed to see what kinds of things merchants had sold in the marketplace and where they had come from—wine, oil, perfume and other exotic things.

As she crept into the pottery room and turned on the light, she reflected that she'd first thought her vessel had contained wine, but further study by an expert in residues had told her that it had contained nothing, which was strange. Pots—jugs, bowls, vessels, amphora and so forth—had been meant to be used. It was unusual to find one that was purely decorative.

The cat had returned. It did not look surprised to see Fiona and moved under the table to wash its face.

Fiona turned the jar around in her hands. The two handles looked the same, but the faint lines where she'd fitted the pieces together had vanished. The twins faced away from the center, arms folded, frowning. And between them, a great gap where the woman had been.

If the twins were still in the picture as well as able to walk around Athens, not to mention pleasure Fiona, did the fact that the demon demigoddess had disappeared mean she was gone?

Best not to jump to conclusions. It might also mean that the twins were still tied to the jar somehow while the demigoddess had escaped it completely.

The fact that all of this was completely impossible made her head ache.

She turned around and saw Pol leaning against the door frame. Fiona gasped and nearly dropped the vessel but caught it at the last minute set it back on the table. The cat meowed as though in disapproval.

"You scared the daylights out of me," Fiona said.

"I move softly." He smiled, the wicked twinkle in place in his eyes as he closed the door and came to her. "I am here before you hear me."

Her skin prickled with his nearness. Cas warmed her all over, but Pol made her hot with curiosity about what he would do.

He gave her a knowing look, waiting.

"Oh gods," she said, realizing. "Was that you I heard in the garden walk near the taverna? When Cas..." She stopped, figuring if it wasn't him, he didn't need to know the details.

Pol took one step closer to her. "When Cas licked your sweet pussy and made you scream, then had you stand up in front of him and make yourself hot?"

"Yes. That's when." She blushed, her face scalding. "You *were* there. I *knew* someone was watching."

"Peace, sweet Fiona." He touched her hair. "'Twas only me, and I enjoyed it very much."

"How completely embarrassing."

He leaned down, his body every bit as warm as Cas' and every bit as exciting. "Why, sweetheart? I loved looking at your ass while you spun your fingers in your honey. I nearly came watching you."

Fiona swallowed hard, feeling that honey flowing once more and just as hot. "Cas said..."

"He said he wanted you to himself. He told me."

She backed one step but the table was behind her, its edge sharp against the backs of her thighs. "So why are you here teasing me?"

"Cas is asleep. No wonder, you wore him out." Pol grinned. "Cas likes different things in a woman than I do. He treats you sweetly, very loving and generous. Pleasuring you and asking nothing for himself."

"I like him."

"Of course you do. Why should you not? But what I like from my women is a little more...obedience."

He threaded his fingers through Fiona's red hair and twisted his hand, not hard, but enough that Fiona would not be able to get away without pulling her hair painfully.

"Obedience," she repeated, her lips numb.

He smiled as though pleased she understood. His black eyes fixed on her, lashes still as he gazed at her steadily.

"For instance, if I found my lady alone in the small hours of the night in her nightdress in a room far from inhabited ones, I would—hmm, now what would I do?" The corners of his mouth quirked in his habitual smile as he thought.

"What?" Fiona faltered.

Pol released her hand and took a step back. His smile remained in place, as wicked as ever. "I'd command her to take off her clothes."

"You would?"

A slow nod. "I would. Take off your clothes, Fiona. Strip for me."

To her consternation, her hand went to the placket of her nightshirt and skimmed it aside to bare her shoulder. "Cas... I told him..."

"Cas is in bed. I am here. I won't usurp his territory — no fucking. He claimed you first and I'll let him have you first. But I want to play."

She bit her lip. "But this is the pottery room."

His smile went feral. "I also have some ideas on what to do when my lady disobeys me."

She shivered as both cold and hot sensations moved through her body. He was a demigod, if she believed in all this. What kinds of things could he do?

Fiona McCarty, whose dissertation on Athenian and Persian amphora won her acclaim, did not strip for men, did not obey them when they smiled like a cat happening upon a mouse they particularly wanted to tease.

No, not a cat, she thought with a glance at the animal washing its face under the table, ignoring them.

Pol was more like a leopard or a panther intent on his prey. His smile was slow, eyes never moving. He knew Fiona would obey, and Fiona knew she would too.

Slowly she eased the wide opening of her nightshirt down her arms, baring her breasts to the harsh light. Pol waited, expression unchanging. She let the nightshirt drop to the floor then she popped open the button of her jeans and slid them down her legs.

A muscle moved in Pol's jaw, but other than that he was a living statue, his body hard under his American School of Classical Studies t-shirt, his cock stiff against the zipper of his jeans.

Fiona slid her underwear down her legs and stepped out of the circle of clothes. There. She was naked except for the sneakers on her feet.

Pol ran his gaze from the top of her head to the tips of her worn shoes. He took his time, raking his sensual gaze slowly from eyes to lips, throat to breasts, belly to quim, thighs to calves. She felt as though someone had touched her physically, warm fingers brushing her skin all the way down.

"Very nice," he pronounced.

She blushed, rather embarrassed by the praise. Archaeologists were quite interested in the open way ancient cultures dealt with sex, but only in erotica of the past. Fiona had never applied her research to herself in the present day.

Pol was a man of that ancient time, when sex was a shared pleasure between two, sometimes more, and not a sin. The archaeologist in her grew excited thinking what a mine of information Cas and Pol could be, a window on the past.

The woman in her grew excited thinking of the kinds of pleasures the people of the past enjoyed and wondering if Pol was about to show her.

"You are beautiful, Fiona, do you know that?"

Cas had called her beautiful too. He'd said it with a deep note in his voice that she'd heard in the voice of art historians when they found a particularly fine statue. She'd loved that he called her beautiful but reminded herself that the garden walk had been dark.

Now she stood under a bare yellow light bulb while Pol let his gaze travel to every part of her.

"Not really," she said, remembering to be bashful.

Pol lost his smile. "I like my ladies to know they are beautiful. Not ashamed of their own bodies. Tell me you are beautiful, Fiona."

Fiona glanced down at herself, at her belly which she thought was too full, at her breasts which could be fuller, fingers that were pudgy and usually coated with dust.

Did any woman ever believe she was beautiful? They were all held to such a high standard even from earliest childhood. *See that woman on the television screen? Now* she's *beautiful.* And if you didn't look like that, you weren't.

Pol's fingers pressed hard to her chin and wrenched her face upward. He'd moved to her so swiftly and silently she was caught off guard. His eyes were sparks of black fury.

"Tell me you are beautiful."

"I am…" The unfamiliar words lodged in her throat.

"Say it." He pinched her chin between hard fingers. "Or I'll whip you."

Her eyes rounded, her heart speeding. In fear or excitement? She couldn't tell. "Whip?"

Pol bent and kissed her. His fingers wove through her hair, pulling her head back, mouth battering and bruising hers.

Her knees weakened, but not for long. Something woke up inside her, something as feral as he was, a long dormant need for wildness and sex and exactly what he was offering.

She wrapped her arms around his neck, fingers biting into his flesh. She opened her mouth wide, wanting all of his tongue and sucking on it when he gave it to her.

When their mouths broke apart, he said, "You love to suck. I like that."

She needed to. She slammed his lips back to hers and got back to the business of sucking on his lips and his tongue. They clutched each other, hands as bruising as mouths, hers skimming to his buttocks under his jeans.

She tried to worm her fingers under his waistband and whimpered in her throat when she couldn't get very far.

Pol wrenched himself away from her. She stumbled a few feet back, panting, watching him round-eyed. He was smiling. He unhooked his belt, also stolen from Hans, and unbuttoned and unzipped the jeans.

He wasn't wearing anything under them. *Going commando*, she thought the expression went. She'd noticed he was bare beneath his jeans in the taverna even while she'd been distracted by Cas' body wrapping around hers.

His cock stood out straight and hard from the black curls of hair framed by the open zipper of the jeans. Dear goddess of love, he looked like the best male magazine model she'd ever seen.

He started laughing, an activity that jiggled the lovely rigid cock up and down. Fiona realized she was staring hard at it, her mouth hanging open, as she waited for Pol to introduce them.

"You've already met," he said, as though reading her mind.

She tried to think of something witty and fun to say but only a strangled noise came out. This was no time for jokes.

Fiona's hand moved of its own accord to rest lightly on the top of his offered cock. "How do you do?" she breathed.

He laughed again, a sound that rumbled through the room and through her body. "How do *you*? Take it in your mouth, Fiona."

The breath went out of her, and her mind darkened with dizziness. Good thing she needed to get on her knees, because she didn't think she could stand any longer.

The warm pile of her clothes cushioned her legs as she sank down in front of Pol, her eyes on that gorgeous cock.

Not too fast, she told herself. *It's like a fabulous piece of chocolate — you start out with a little taste, a little nibble to sate your craving and tempt yourself at the same time, and then you really dig in.*

Savor this.

Fiona leaned forward slightly as Pol stepped close to her. He held his jeans by the waistband, the opening hanging loose, the belt dragging the fabric to either side. His cock had to be eleven inches to a foot long—there were measuring tools in the pottery room, maybe she should…

Later. After she'd enjoyed it for a while. His hair was so black, shining in the light, his cock smelling a little like dust and velvet. She nuzzled the tip and was rewarded by his smooth skin bumping her nose.

"Mmm," he said appreciatively.

She ran the tip of her nose around him playfully then put out her tongue and touched it to his slit. His knuckles went white where he clutched the fabric of the jeans, sinews in his forearms moving.

Fiona wriggled her tongue over his slit some more, tasting the bead of moisture that had welled up at her touch. She dragged her tongue around his flange, rubbing the small line of flesh under the tip.

"Baby, what are you doing to me?" he said, his voice roughening.

"Having fun," Fiona said. She sucked his tip into her mouth then pushed it out again right away.

"Cruel woman."

"I'm the one obeying you," she pointed out. Before he could answer, she drew his cock all the way into her mouth.

"That's it," he whispered. He unballed one fist and dragged his fingers through her hair.

Fiona grasped his buttocks, sinking her fingers into his skin, and went to work on his cock.

She drew back, letting it fall out of her mouth, blowing a little on it. She had no idea where this playful, sex-crazed woman inside her had come from. Sex to her had always been more or less an obligation to please a man so she wouldn't be alone.

Pathetic. It wasn't like she hadn't *wanted* sex and sexual pleasure, but her friends had always told her that sex was what you had to do to keep men happy. They weren't good enough at it to keep you happy, so you either had to keep yourself happy or find a girlfriend who knew how to.

Because Fiona had been too self-conscious to touch herself, and never had any interest in other women, she'd assumed that sex was all right but nothing special.

Cas had begun teaching her that sexual pleasure could be the most outstanding thing on the planet, and Pol was busy hammering the point home. Cas, with his warm eyes and rare smile, was already stealing her heart.

His brother Pol was a lover of a different kind. Demanding, for one thing.

"Harder." His hand twisted in her hair.

She obeyed. She slid his cock back into her mouth and rolled her tongue all over it while she sucked. He tasted so good, warm and salty and *male*. Her entire body tingled with the maleness of him.

"Ah, Fiona." The words dragged out of him, a man obviously happy with what she was doing. He rocked slightly on his heels, pressing himself deeper into her mouth.

She loved every different taste of him. The rough texture and spicy taste of the base of him, the smooth, honey-sweetness of his tip, the rigid and satin taste of his flange. She liked licking his balls too, she discovered, smooth skin covered with wiry hair.

His balls rode high and tight, round and almost as hard as his cock. Experimentally she drew one into her mouth and lightly grazed it with her teeth.

"*Damn.*"

"Do you like that?" she asked.

"Do I *like* it?" He pushed her back toward the base of his cock. "What is that telling you?"

"You like it." She laughed in delight. How pleasing it was to please a man who really liked to be pleased. She laughed again at her tongue-twisting thoughts.

Fiona teased and licked and nibbled at his balls a little longer, then went back to the satisfying feast of his cock.

Pol had begun their encounter in control, but by the way his hands alternately flexed and closed and tugged at her hair or pulled her farther onto him, he had left control behind.

"Fiona, sweet goddess."

She licked him harder, nibbling the sensitive underside of his tip. The twins had it fixed in their heads that she was a goddess who'd used her special magic to rescue them. They were completely wrong, but it was rather fun to be an object of fascination and desire.

"I'm going to come," he moaned.

His strong hands tightened in her hair, holding her to him while he rocked into her mouth. Fiona had never swallowed a man down before and had no clue what to expect.

Pol growled low in his throat, his hips moving, and then smooth, thick liquid filled her mouth. She ran her tongue through it and swallowed, liking the strange new taste.

The seed of a demigod. Plain Fiona had come a long way.

Pol hauled her to her feet and gathered her close. His body shuddered and he buried his face in her neck. The feel of his t-shirt and still-open jeans on her bare skin excited her, and she kissed him.

He held her hard, kissing her back, the taste of his seed and his tongue mixing together into a heady cocktail.

"Fiona," he whispered. "Thank you." He kissed her again, his tongue a rough weight in her mouth.

"Thank you," he repeated, and she had the feeling that his thanks went beyond her pleasuring him. "Thank you, sweet Fiona."

Chapter Seven

ဢ

How can they leave a trail ten feet wide, Selena fumed, *and then disappear?*

It had been easy to trace Cas and Pol through the previous day and night—everyone remembered the tall, unbelievably handsome twins and their devilish smiles.

Probably charming their way into getting everyone to do exactly what they want.

While she could respect getting people to obey, she couldn't respect the method. Pain was so much more effective.

At least, it used to be. The twins must retain some of their powers, because they kept eluding Selena, always having just left a place she entered. She would get turned around on the back streets and the people there would remember the twins but not quite which direction they went.

It was enough to drive a demon demigoddess crazy.

Finally, after they'd left the last restaurant in the wee hours of the morning, she hadn't been able to trace them. She'd returned to her slave in his tiny apartment and whipped him senseless to relieve her pique.

In the morning, he still lay groaning on the floor. She stepped over him on the way out, not bothering to yank him to his feet. She didn't need him anymore anyway.

Angry and hungry, Selena approached a stand selling the tasty beverage called coffee. It pleased her that she could make the vendor give her the coffee without payment simply by glaring at him. She hadn't lost her touch entirely.

She felt stronger this morning, as though her powers were slowly returning. Maybe it was all the fucking she'd done with the peasant man. He was used up though. She'd have to find another one.

That the twins still eluded her made her boil with rage. She couldn't follow them — they'd obviously left magic behind to confuse her — so she needed to get one step ahead of them.

How, she didn't know.

She needed to find the damn jar and try to get them back into it. This time, she'd make sure the spell worked, and they'd bury themselves deep in her forever.

Mmm, what a lovely thought. Pol and Cas huge and hard inside her and never able to get out. Never able to release although *she* would release and grow excited as many times as she wanted.

She looked over the magazines and newspapers at a stand next to the coffee vendor's. Politics of the time, salacious gossip about people she'd never heard of. Boring, boring, boring.

Her attention was arrested by a magazine in the corner, dog-eared and forlorn, like no one wanted it. But on the cover, bold as could be, was a picture of her jar.

She pointed a red talon at it. "Give me that."

"The archaeology magazine?" the vendor looked bewildered. "You don't look the type."

Selena grabbed the man's shirtfront and jerked him down to his glossy copies of nude and sports magazines. "I said, *give it to me.*"

Coughing, the vendor grabbed the magazine, shoved it at her and backed to the farthest corner of his stall. Ignoring him, Selena walked away, flipping through the magazine until she found the article she wanted.

There was the jar, chipped and half-finished. But those men were Cas and Pol, naked and beautiful, and there was herself, beautiful too, hanging between them. Their cocks were half buried in her.

Should have been, anyway.

She skimmed the article, her brain already adapted to twenty-first century Greek. What she read raised her anger to blazing fury.

Selena slammed the magazine closed, holding the place with her finger. She waited until one of the taxis sped toward her, then she stepped out in front of it.

It screeched to a halt as though stopped by a giant force. The driver leaned out of the window, staring at her with round eyes, his face white.

Selena jerked open the passenger door and climbed in beside him. "Do you know where this is?"

She opened the magazine and jammed her pointed nail at the paragraph that told her the jar was being studied by a postdoc fellow at the American School of Classical Studies in Athens.

"It's in the Kolonaki District," the man stammered.

"Good. Take me there. *Now.*"

The driver gulped, jammed his foot to the floor and swerved the vehicle out into traffic.

* * * * *

Fiona rose in her usual morning fog, stumbled to the showers with her towel and toothbrush, mumbled good morning to the other women in the bathroom, and stepped under the lukewarm water to wash her hair.

When the slap of shampoo woke her up, she froze, suds dripping down her face, as she remembered.

She had freed two demigods, chased them across Athens, let them fondle her, then went with them one at a time to pleasure and be pleasured by them.

She'd done it with *twins*.

Twins who still had Hans Jorgensen's clothes and credit cards and the gods only knew what they'd get up to today.

Fiona hurried through her ablutions, zipped a towel over her skin and pulled her clothes over her still-damp body. She skimmed a toothbrush over her teeth then dashed out of the dorm to make her way to the Agora.

When she got to the dig, it teemed with people. They all seemed to congregate on the northwest side, standing in the stance that Fiona had come to recognize as archaeologists excited, hands on hips or fingers to chins, all staring quietly down at the same spot as though hoping and not wanting to hope that here was a great find.

In the front of the group was Cas and Pol and Hans Jorgensen. Fiona pushed her way through, breathing "excuse me" half a dozen times before she got through bodies to the front of the crowd.

Pol looked her way and gave her a wink. Her blush return and flared even more when Cas sent her a slow smile.

Hans and the rest of the archaeologists paid no attention. Hans was scraping his blond hair back with agitated hands as he stared at the lump of stone that had been revealed in the earth.

He glanced at Fiona and his eyes widened. "Fiona, do you know what they have done?"

Fiona flinched, expecting him to chastise her for allowing them to steal his credit cards, but Hans went on before she could interrupt.

"They have found a *stoa*. One not known of before. They brought me to it—it will make my career if it is true what they say."

"They minted coin here," Cas said. "There is a room and coins still there. Worth much money to you, I imagine."

Hans stared at him as though he'd grown three heads. "Money? I suppose. But a previously unknown *stoa*... Thank you, my good friends. I must mark the spot and make a sketch..." He squatted in the dirt and started examining the ground minutely as though forgetting that anyone else was nearby.

The others either congratulated him and moved off to their own jobs or stayed to help him. Fiona glanced at Hans' big body and rapt face then switched her gaze to the twins, who looked back at her, grinning.

She glared at them, turned around and walked away.

If she thought they were going to follow her and apologize, she was wrong. She stomped most of the way through the Agora before she realized they'd stayed with Hans.

"Men," she said through clenched teeth, not sure why she was angry at the whole sex.

"I thought you were more interested in pottery than spectacular finds," Joan Whittington said in passing.

"I am." Fiona made her way back to the pottery room before Joan could continue. Let the woman think she was jealous of Hans. She had too much going on to worry about it.

She had come here last night to research the problem of the jar and why Pol and Cas remained depicted on it while the demigoddess was not. And then Pol had come in telling her to take off her clothes and had started unzipping his jeans.

The memory of the smooth taste of his come made her heat up again, her blood firing in her veins.

Research, she told herself. *Focus on research.*

She pulled out books and journals she'd collected on ancient Greek pottery and concentrated on those of the fifth century B.C.E., the height of the Athenian empire and the time of Pericles. She'd already combed these books for information on jars similar to her own and found little, but she might have missed something.

She'd have to go to the school and look through their library for legends of Castor and Pollux and Gemini. Greek gods usually had more than one story told about them, more than one facet.

Zeus, for example, though he was the king of the gods, had other aspects that were worshiped at different times. In the temple in the Agora, Zeus was worshiped in his aspect as counselor, which made sense because the senate and law courts had met nearby.

Castor and Pollux might appear in some lore and legends that were unknown in the present day. Fiona was historian enough to know that what archaeologists knew of the past was the tip of the iceberg and that so much was forever lost. *Somewhere* there must be the story of the jar and the magic that went along with it.

Fiona picked out the books that might be most helpful and hoisted them into her backpack. She trotted back down to the dig, where Hans was sketching the area and Cas and Pol were holding forth on what he would find.

Cas and Pol were two fabulously built men. With the sun on their black hair, their skin bronzed and clothes stretched over tight bodies, they could easily make next year's *He-Men of Archaeology* calendar.

When they caught sight of her, they broke off and sauntered toward her. Her mouth went dry as they both sent her looks of hot promise, both of them reminding her of what they'd done in secret last night. Sheesh, when had her life become so complicated?

They moved to either side of her, Cas on the right, Pol on the left, their body heat enclosing hers.

Pol touched the backpack slung over her shoulder. "You are going somewhere?"

"Yes, to the library."

She expected them to tell her they would accompany her and perhaps stop off in a taverna for wine and more touching, but Cas said, "We will stay here and help Hans."

"What did you tell him? How did you get him to believe you knew of a completely new and undisturbed find?"

"I said that we had been here for a dig many years ago," Cas answered. "That they had uncovered a little of the new *stoa*, but had not been able to—what is the word for your magic?—*excavate* it."

"And he believed that?"

"Not at first," Pol said. "Not until we showed him where the first stone was. Then he did not care how we had found it. The prospect of a few stones excited him more than the thousands of coins that lie beneath it."

Fiona pressed a hand to her forehead. "This is what you meant when you said you'd pay him back."

"Yes," Cas answered. "There are many more coins here than what a meal and wine and transport cost us yesterday."

"True, but…" She bit her lip. "You *did* tell him about the credit card business, right?"

"We did," Pol said, warm amusement in his eyes. "After we showed him the *stoa*. He said not to bother about it, we had more than paid him back."

She looked back and forth between them, sensing the smugness radiating from both. "I can't believe you two."

"Why not?" Cas' mouth quirked, but his gaze moved over Fiona like a touch. "We have made Hans Jorgensen very, very happy. He said he owed us his life, which of course we will not take. It is quite dangerous to say that to a demigod."

"I'll be certain and remind him," she said faintly.

"We are the demigods of good times," Pol said, his gaze and smile as devastating as his brother's. "Not wrathful or vengeful. But speaking of gods of good times, I wonder why Dionysus has not tried to find us. We have gone to the places he would linger and have seen nothing of him."

"There is a temple to Athena above us," Cas said, his gaze moving to the Parthenon on the flat hill.

Streams of tourists in many-colored shirts streamed up the hill toward the temple, but even with that modernity, the pillars standing on the Acropolis, the *ancientness* of it, overwhelmed tourists in t-shirts with cell-phones and cameras.

"But they are abandoned and ruined," Cas went on, a note of sadness entering his voice. "The gods no longer come here to smell the burned offerings or hear the prayers of their people. They've gone."

"They couldn't have gone completely," Pol argued. "They loved this land and the people in it."

Cas gave him a somber look. "I do not feel them here. There are new religions and new beliefs, and the gods have been forgotten."

Pol looked as though he wanted to argue further, but Fiona broke in. "Cas is right. Everyone is fascinated by the gods, but they don't believe in them any longer. There are still people who call on them, but very few."

Cas turned his head to look over the Agora, the sun glistening on his dark hair, looking very much a god. The sorrow of his loss touched her, making her heart sting with grief for him.

"Well, I am going to find out what happened to you," she announced. "Why you were trapped in oblivion and if there's any danger of you going back."

Both swung to her, their gazes glittering. The cords in Pol's neck tightened. "What do you mean? There is danger of us returning to — to nothingness?"

"I don't know. The picture changed and the demigoddess disappeared, but you did not. I don't know whether that means she died or you are only partially free, or if it means nothing. That's why I'm going to the library, to find out and to try to free you all the way if you aren't."

The twins glanced at one another. She saw a ripple of uneasiness between them, fear that they did not want to admit.

"Fiona," Cas said. His eyes were dark as he softly touched her face. "You are good to use your magic to help us. I do not fully understand why you do this, but we are grateful."

Fiona shrugged, trying to be offhand, but her throat tightened.

If she were to lose Pol and Cas to whatever magic had trapped them before, she would be more than sorry. She'd known them only a little longer than twenty-four hours, but they had awakened in her something no other man—or men—had.

Besides, she liked them. They were troublemakers, that was apparent, but they bore no animosity to anyone.

"I hope I can help," she said, not knowing how to respond. "I'll do my best."

Pol growled. "If the gods would show their faces, we could get some answers from them. Apollo has a temple in the Agora, so do Zeus and Athena. People may have abandoned them, but they have abandoned their places as well."

"Well, I don't know how to talk to gods, but I *do* know how to talk to librarians." Fiona held up her hands, palm outward. "You will *stay here*, right?"

Pol exchanged another glance with Cas, which worried her, but his voice was perfectly steady when he answered. "Of course. We will help Hans. He seems personable. And when you return…"

He lowered his left eyelid in a wink. Behind him, Cas sent her a knowing smile. *We'll play when we're all together*, he seemed to say, *but when you and I are alone…*

Fiona hastily turned on her heel and left them before she succumbed to the heady visions in her head and dragged them both of to her room to see what they had in mind.

* * * * *

The library yielded only a few interesting pieces of information. There were many versions of the story of Pol grieving for Cas' death and sharing his immortality until Zeus made them both immortal.

She read that they'd had adventures with Jason and the Argonauts—it took little stretch of the imagination to picture them sailing from port to port, fighting monsters, having women and enjoying every moment of it.

Castor was supposed to be an excellent horseman, Pol a boxer, which also went with the twins she knew. A person had to have quiet strength and patience to do well with horses, and boxers needed a combination of aggression and cunning. Pollux had apparently been able to kill with his boxing skills.

Some stories said that they hatched from the same egg, some from two eggs, some that they had different fathers, Leda's mortal husband and Zeus.

All the stories agreed that they were identical, powerful, fun-loving and close. *The demigods of good times*, they called themselves.

Only one story was a little different. Castor and Pollux were pursued by a demon demigoddess who was so adamant to have them she sent a hydra to capture them, but whether the hydra succeeded, the story didn't say.

Fiona sighed and closed her last book. There might be more about the jar in libraries back at the University of Chicago, and she'd have to search the Internet and the email loops in case an archaeologist was working on something that could help her.

The library was quiet today, most people out either doing their jobs or taking vacation on the coast. She sat in a shadowed corner near a window with a long stretch of empty tables and chairs between her and the door.

Except now they weren't empty. A woman lounged in a chair not far from her. She had long black hair that swept to her lap in a sensuous wave and wore tight black leather pants and a black leather bustier, impractical for the hot weather of summer, and strange attire for an academic library.

When Fiona stood up, the woman smiled and stood up too. She had a pointed face, dark eyes and a full-lipped, scarlet mouth. She wore gloves on her hands and carried a whip coiled in one fist.

Fiona looked into the woman's face and gasped, the sound loud in the quiet library.

Her eyes were black pools of evil, eroticism taken in a foul direction, sex used for pain and torture and death. She was a woman who got her pleasure using people until they begged to get away, and then she punished them for pleading for mercy and killed them anyway.

Fiona sensed all that behind the woman's eyes, a sticky, foul malevolence that soiled the air of the innocent library.

"So," the woman said, her deep voice filled with scorn. "You took away my boys."

"You're the demigoddess," Fiona whispered.

"I am Selena." Her bosom mounded high over the bustier. "The twins belong to me."

"Not anymore, they don't," Fiona said quickly. The woman was scary as hell, but Fiona had no intention of letting Pol and Cas back under her power. Selena had deprived them of twenty-five hundred years of their life until they woke up in a world they didn't understand.

Selena cocked her head, studying Fiona closely. "You must have great magic to be able to lift the spell. As much as you lifted it, anyway."

Fiona automatically started to deny that she had any powers at all, then reconsidered. It wouldn't hurt if this woman believed she wasn't as defenseless as she felt.

"I have the magic of archaeology," Fiona said, drawing herself up. "I used it to free Cas and Pol."

"Lucky them." The woman ran her gloved fingers over her own lips, outlining her blood-red mouth. "If I wasn't so pissed off at you, I'd do you sweetly, my dear. I'd be nice, since you're so pretty."

A shiver of loathing went through Fiona. "Why did you bind them to the jar? How did you do it? It was a clever bit of sorcery."

The woman slanted her a smile that said she'd caught on to Fiona's attempt at flattery.

"It wasn't clever at all, just a simple binding spell. We performed the ritual that you saw so nicely painted on your jar. And then we became a part of it, to have raw, beautiful sex forever." She waved her fingers, looking triumphant.

"But something went wrong," Fiona said. "The twins were in oblivion, and I'm willing to bet you were too."

Rage flared in Selena's black eyes and sparks actually shot from them, making Fiona take several hasty steps back.

"Interfering bitch wouldn't let me have my fun," Selena hissed.

"Which bitch?"

Selena opened her mouth to answer then smiled again. "Oh no, I'm not giving you all my secrets."

"At least tell me why you are no longer pictured on the jar while they are."

Selena smirked. "Wouldn't you like to know? There's nothing you can do, darling, Castor and Pollux will be forever connected with that piece of clay. After I entered the spell, I had one of my slaves break the jar and scatter the pieces far and wide so the goddesses they'd beguiled wouldn't be able to find it. Lazy bitches wouldn't bother to look if there was a chance they'd break a nail."

"Good thing I persisted in finding it," Fiona pointed out. "Or else you'd be trapped in oblivion still."

"The oblivion thing was a *slight* complication." Selena made a tiny space between gloved thumb and forefinger. "But now that all the goddesses have abandoned this place, I can do my spell again. Ah, sweet eternity with those two enormous, gorgeous cocks buried in my body." She closed her eyes and gave a little shiver.

"Cas and Pol don't belong to you," Fiona said angrily.

Selena's eyes snapped open. "They don't belong to *you*, sweetie. I don't care how much they've stroked and teased you." Her smile returned as Fiona blushed. "They have, haven't they? They can't keep their hands off anything female. Did they make you believe you're special to them?" She imitated a pout. "Isn't that *sweet*, they made you think they cared."

Fiona felt an answering fury bubble deep inside her. This woman, for all her power and eroticism, knew nothing about Cas and Pol, cared nothing about them.

"Get out of here," she said, finding strength in anger. "You don't belong here."

Her voice rang to the very corners of the library. The shelves and shelves of books lining the walls seemed to frown, not liking the noise, yet agreeing that the black-haired woman had to go.

Instantly, Selena was at Fiona's side, long fingers twisting in Fiona's hair. She laid the coiled whip against Fiona's cheek. "Stupid little bitch, your magic is *nothing* compared to mine. I am a demigoddess, daughter of Poseidon. Do you think you can challenge me?"

No, Fiona really didn't. If she hadn't already talked herself into believing magic had trapped Cas and Pol for twenty-five hundred years, she'd believe it now. The woman radiated power—harsh, evil power—and Fiona knew Selena could kill her here and now. There was nothing Fiona could do to stop her.

Fiona felt something brush her lower leg, then a gray tabby cat with orange eyes, looking remarkably like the one that liked to hang around the dig, jumped to the nearest table. It glared at Selena, slammed its ears back and hissed.

Selena swung around and slashed at the cat with her whip.

Except the cat wasn't there. The air shimmered with energy where the cat had been, energy that vibrated up the whip and slammed Selena hard into a table behind her.

Selena climbed to her feet, blinking. *I should run,* Fiona thought, but her feet were frozen to the floor, her limbs unable to move.

And then the cat was back on the table, its hackles raised, its orange glare trained on Selena.

"Bitch!" Selena screamed at it. She started backing away, navigating the chairs and tables with difficulty, no longer trying to lash out with the whip. "You won't be able to protect her always. And you —" She switched her furious gaze to Fiona, stabbing the air with a leather-covered finger. "You won't be able to protect *them.* Think about what might happen if that jar breaks."

Fiona's eyes widened. She pictured her jar sitting unprotected in the pottery room and a stray archaeologist bumping the table and sending the vessel to the cement floor. She imagined the pictures of Pol and Cas lying broken and splintered.

Did Selena mean they would die? Or be sent back to oblivion? And what was to stop Selena from rushing to the dig and breaking the jar herself?

Fiona made a noise in her throat. The cat lashed its tail, still glaring at Selena. The black-clad woman sneered one last time then turned and strode off, disappearing in mid-air.

Fiona shuddered, released from her frozen stance. She glanced at the cat, who yawned, then sat on its haunches and began washing its face in a very catlike manner.

"Thank you," Fiona told it. "Whoever you are, thank you for stopping her."

The cat continued to wash its face as though oblivious to human chatter.

Tentatively, Fiona rubbed it between the ears, hoping that she wasn't offending whatever entity was inside. The cat lowered its paw and leaned against Fiona's hand, its body rumbling with purrs.

"Really, thank you." Fiona dragged in a breath, fear bringing her strength back. "I have to go. I have to make sure she doesn't hurt Cas and Pol."

The cat rubbed its head against her hand a few more times. Then it jumped down from the table and stalked away, tail straight in the air, looking smug as only a cat could.

* * * * *

The transport called a *motorcycle* was hard to get used to, but after only a few mishaps Cas began to catch on. He had to admit he enjoyed the curses he drew from his brother who clung on behind him.

They'd gotten the motorcycle from Hans Jorgensen who'd good naturedly told them to take it and enjoy their trip. They'd gotten the map of modern Greece from a man in the flea market and the whole idea of the trip from Hans.

"Does anyone worship the gods any longer?" Pol had asked him that morning. "Anyone at all?"

Hans had actually paused in his joy of brushing dust from stones to answer them. "When visiting Mount Olympus earlier this summer, I met people who kept shrines to the old gods. I had much interesting conversation with them."

"Mount Olympus, of course." Pol's eyes shone with anticipation. "We will go, perhaps in one of the things you call taxis."

Hans laughed. "That would cost a fortune if they would even go. You need to take a bus or the train. Or you could borrow my bike. I am not going anywhere for a while." He gave the stone floor a look most men reserved for their lovers. "And I give much thanks to you for it."

Cas and Pol mounted the bike, which seemed to be a mechanical horse with wheels, listened to brief instruction from Hans how to start it, then jammed helmets on their heads and took off.

Dr. Wheelan's voice trailed after them as they rode out of the compound, "You do have a license to operate a motorcycle, don't you?" At least that's what Cas thought he said. It was difficult to understand him over the roaring of the bike.

Chapter Eight

❧

Cas' magic could move people aside for him if he had to, without the people in question being aware he'd passed. But on the bike, he didn't need to use his magic. The other vehicles dove hastily out of the way as Cas raced through the streets, the drivers of them shouting and waving. Cas waved back and kept going.

He hadn't understood the map of confusing byways through town, but he didn't really need it. He was a demigod, and all gods were drawn to Mount Olympus. They weren't always welcome there, but they were drawn.

Cas unerringly drove north and west, finding a route out of the city after a long time of maneuvering through it.

There was no definite gate or boundary to mark the edge of Athens as there had been in his time. The buildings upon buildings simply dwindled and fell away, and at last they were racing through open countryside—rolling hills and deep river valleys leading to sharp mountains.

Pol stopped cursing behind him and settled down to enjoy the scenery. There was still traffic, but not as much, and the roads were unbelievably smooth. They roared through villages—clusters of white-washed houses with blue painted shutters and doors—and out again, the traffic becoming more sparse as they went.

A couple of times, soldiers called *police* waved them to stop and demanded of Cas why he was driving so swiftly. While Cas talked, Pol soothed these soldiers' minds so they forgot why they'd stopped and that they'd threatened to take Cas and Pol to jail.

Once the soldiers became friendly, they pointed out the roads to take to reach Mount Olympus in a shorter time and invited them to stop at their friends' or families' homes or cafés for a meal and wine. They also explained about something called *petrol* or *gasoline* that they needed to feed the motorcycle in order to keep it going.

Cas and Pol did stop once or twice when they got hungry, and spent a few hours drinking and telling stories with large families who wouldn't let them go without a promise of a visit on return. The people at the places where they found the gasoline also pressed gifts of food and fizzy *soft drinks* on them.

Cas brought the blessings of the gods onto all their houses, ensuring that they'd be wealthy and fruitful, and then he and Pol went on their way.

They rode for a long time, well after the sun set and the world went dark. Above them, thousands upon thousands of stars stretched across the horizon, white smudges in the dark.

Cas knew the constellations like old friends, but there were new stars up there, several of which moved. He knew now about *airplanes*, those vehicles that flew in the sky and transported people from country to country in a matter of hours, but these lights were tiny and distant. He'd have to ask Fiona about them.

Busy gazing at these new moving stars, he ran the bike into a ditch, throwing Pol and himself off to land in a pasture of startled sheep. Thinking they might as well rest, Cas pulled the bike from the ditch, removed his helmet and brought out the packets of pita bread and *souvlakia* that the women at the last house had pressed on them to take for the journey.

Pol was cursing as soon as his helmet was off. "I learned a new phrase from the Americans at the dig. Your driving *sucks*."

"What does that mean exactly?" Cas stretched out on the bank and chewed on well-seasoned chicken in bread.

"Technically, it's what a woman does to a man's cock. But it has taken on the meaning that someone does something badly. Really, really badly."

"Fiona doesn't do it badly." Cas slanted a glance as his brother. "Does she?"

Pol's anger softened into his usual grin. "You saw? She is a goddess and does everything as a goddess should."

"Of course I saw. I can't stay away from her. Neither can you."

"She is fetching, you must admit." Pol opened his own packet of meat and bread and *tzatzíki* and began to eat.

Cas watched Pol for a while, then said slowly. "I claim her."

"I know." Pol chewed and swallowed and looked up at the stars. "You've lost your heart, haven't you?"

"I have."

"'Tis the way to disaster, Cas. Lovers come to grief, like Aphrodite and Adonis."

Cas snorted. "That story does not mean *lovers come to grief*. It means *always listen when a goddess tells you you'll die if you go hunting that day*. Adonis was an idiot."

"That is true. I already told Fiona I'd back off and let you have her first. Don't say I never did anything for you."

Cas finished his meal in silence and lay back to watch the stars. A stream trickled somewhere nearby, the rushing sound soothing. He hadn't felt jealousy when he'd entered the pottery room and seen Fiona, nude and lush, on her knees with her sweet mouth around Pol's cock.

He'd felt a rush of desire and his own cock had hardened. She'd done so well licking and nipping and suckling that he'd almost felt it all the way across the room. Pol made her laugh, which meant her red mouth was smiling, her eyes glowing in delight.

Suck him, love, that's it, had gone through his mind. He wanted her for himself, but the joy of watching her was heady and hard to resist. He wanted to fuck her and love her, but he wanted to watch Pol fuck her afterward.

A plan began to form in his head.

Pol licked the last of the *tzatzíki* off his fingers. "Keep going?" he asked. "Or sleep?"

Cas climbed to his feet and reached for his helmet. "Keep going."

Demigods didn't need sleep like humans did, and he still hadn't shaken off the pall of being in oblivion for twenty-five hundred years. He hoped they could find Zeus or Dionysus or Apollo, and that the gods would fill them in on all they had missed.

It took them another three hours to reach Mount Olympus, and they drove through the town of Litohoro at its base in the pitch dark. The headlight on the bike led them along a paved road for a while, which soon turned to rutted dirt. When the track became too narrow and rocky, they left the bike and proceeded on foot.

At least Cas knew where he was. The foothills of the mountain had always been dominated by humans who ventured as high as they dared to seek the gods and their wisdom and help. They weren't always welcome. The gods had plenty of sudden snowstorms at their disposal—even in high summer—to throw at unwanted visitors.

The track became precarious, especially in the dark, but Cas walked along without worry, Pol tramping close behind him.

The sat down to rest high on the slopes, the frigid air chilling them. They waited without speaking, perched on boulders by a fold of valley through which ran a noisy stream.

The sun rose slowly, light spilling into the river valley and turning the air to mist. Through the mist, a stag wandered to the stream, its antlers huge and intricate, indicating he'd survived many a season. The stag lowered his head to the stream and drank.

Cas rose to his feet. The stag started and looked up at him, water streaming from its mouth.

Pol got up as well, and the stag turned to run, frightened by the humans intruding on his world.

"We see you," Cas said. He lifted a bottle that had been pressed on him by one of the families along the journey. "I brought the wine this time. Remember? I promised."

The stag stopped. It stood looking at them for a long time then it began walking toward them. In a particularly thick patch of mist the stag blurred into the form of a large, muscular human, the antlers remaining on his head.

"But I always bring the wine," Dionysus said as he spread his hand.

A feast laid itself out on a cloth of gold at the twins' feet, plates of meat and pastries, overflowing bowls of grapes and huge golden goblets of wine.

The god walked around the feast and clasped Cas' hand between his two huge ones. "Well met," he said formally.

Then suddenly he roared with laughter and grabbed Cas in a crushing bear hug. "I should say, *where the hell have you been?*"

* * * * *

Fiona drove northward toward Thrace both steaming mad and cold with worry. In the front seat of the tiny car she'd rented lay the vessel, wrapped in sheets and pillows to cushion the ride.

Technically, she should not take the jar from the dig — all the finds belonged to Greece, and there was still a lot of tension over the Elgin Marbles, which had been looted from the Parthenon two hundred years ago and resided in England. She justified her theft by telling herself she wasn't taking the vessel out of Greece, and she feared it would be broken or lost if she kept it at the dig.

When Hans had explained that Cas and Pol had not only gone off to Mount Olympus but had taken Hans' motorcycle, she'd put her hands to her head and groaned.

The gray cat, the one that looked remarkably like the cat in the library, had rubbed her ankles at that moment. Fiona knew she had to go after them. They were demigods and could probably take care of themselves, but the menace in Selena's threats was real and she had power.

If it hadn't been for the cat…

First I have demigods coming out of a painted jar and having sex with me, and then a cat saves my life from a demon demigoddess.

Who was the cat? Another demigoddess? Which one?

I'm drowning in mythology.

Two things were certain — Fiona had to warn the twins that Selena was free and raring to go and that they had to protect the jar at all costs.

117

She took the most direct route possible to Litohoro and hoped the twins hadn't detoured to drink and dance the night away in some village on the other side of the Greek mainland. But as Athens fell farther and farther behind, she had no trouble getting answers to her faulty Greek questions about two handsome men on a motorcycle. The twins had been remembered far and wide.

Some people were furious at them—she heard garbled accusations of upset sheep and hens that wouldn't lay—and some laughed and remembered them fondly. Either way, she knew she was on the right trail.

A man in Litohoro remembered a motorcycle tearing through earlier that night, but by then Fiona was too exhausted to drive any farther. Plus she knew she'd never navigate narrow mountain roads in the dark.

She found a tiny inn off the road that was willing to take in a stray American at two in the morning. She kept the jar at her side all night, only half-sleeping in case Selena showed up and tried to wrestle it from her.

Morning dawned without any drama, and Fiona downed a tiny cup of thick coffee and drove off, the jar beside her, to Mount Olympus. The mountain was a favorite hiking trek of tourists, so her car joined many others at the end of a paved road that led to the trails.

She looked up the craggy slopes and high cliffs of the mountain, the top bathed in mist. The helpful map she'd picked up in the town showed several routes to the summit, all of them for hardy hikers with the right supplies. All Fiona had was sandals and an ancient jar wrapped in a sheet.

Without any clear idea how she would find the twins or even if she could, Fiona started to walk.

After two hours she was out of breath and her legs hurt. She ground her teeth and wondered what she was doing there. She should just go back to Litohoro and wait for the twins to come down.

She stopped to rest, leaning on a flat rock on the side of the hill, looking down the trail into a misty gorge. A few hikers went past her, hardy types who chatted to each other cheerfully as they went by, not even breathing hard.

"This is stupid," she muttered. "I'll never find them. I'm going back."

As she uttered the words she grew suddenly dizzy, so dizzy she thought she'd heave out her breakfast of too-strong coffee. She couldn't have altitude sickness, she reasoned, because the last marker indicated that she'd reached eight-hundred meters, which was only about twenty-four hundred feet.

Nor could she have a hangover, because she hadn't drunk anything but bottled water the night before. Of course, it could always be a nasty virus or food poisoning. As her mind went down this happy trail, her vision went entirely black.

Just as suddenly it cleared. She was standing in a completely different part of the mountain in a meadow of bright red and blue flowers bisected by a wide stream. The slopes of Mount Olympus cascaded *down* from where she was, which didn't make any sense, unless she'd climbed to the top in her sleep.

All the hikers had disappeared, but near the stream, lying on their asses on a cloth of gold like they were having a great time, were Cas and Pol.

She was so relieved to see them that at first she didn't notice the third figure.

For a moment, she viewed things her mind could not comprehend. She thought she saw a man, huge and nude and perfectly formed, but with an elegant set of antlers rising from his head as though they were completely natural. He seemed to move in shadow, and she was reminded of descriptions of the Celtic horned god—the god of harvest and fertility, the lover and husband of the Goddess.

But this was modern Greece not ancient Britain, and the gods were myths.

At least that's what she'd thought before Cas and Pol had appeared in her bed two nights ago.

The god seemed to shimmer and grow smaller, and then he was just a man with a loincloth draped about his hips. The antlers disappeared, although whenever he turned his head too quickly, she saw the vaguest hint of them above his ears.

As she walked toward the trio, she became more and more uncertain she'd seen anything godlike. Perhaps he was a hermit or one of the monks from the monasteries that dotted this part of Greece. Not that she expected monks to walk around mostly naked, but perhaps he'd taken his vow of poverty to the extreme.

Cas rose as she neared them. He opened his arms to her and then everything was all right. His warmth enveloped her like a blanket, his scent scattered her thoughts and his lips in her hair made her anger and fear evaporate.

She handed the jar to Pol and concentrated on hugging Cas. He snaked his hand down to her backside and hauled her up for a long, tongue-tangling kiss.

"Mmm," she said as they parted. "I guess you missed me."

"I did too, sweetheart," Pol said, running a warm hand over her backside.

Still in Cas' arms, Fiona turned her head and kissed Pol on the lips, her insides tingling with wickedness and wanting.

"This is the woman who freed you?"

The third man spoke English, but with a rich, deep accent that would make the most frigid of women strip off her clothes and spread herself in front of him. She'd beg him to take her hard and fast and not worry about being gentle. Fiona's hand even went to the first button of her blouse before she could stop it.

Cas twined his arm firmly around her waist and the compulsion suddenly faded. That is, she no longer wanted to strip for the third man. She wanted to strip for Pol and Cas.

Cas kissed her temple. "This is Fiona."

The third man looked her up and down. He was a breathtaking portrait of the perfectly shaped man, broad shoulders, knotted muscles, hard chest, pectorals flat and defined without being overly bulgy, biceps smooth and firm, abdomen flat, thighs taut.

He had brown-black eyes that swam with flecks of gold, and his hair was midnight black like Cas' and Pol's. A gold band circled his upper arm, the designs on it Greek, but very, very old.

As an ordinary man, he would have been spectacular. But Fiona felt the immense power in him, a strange magic that radiated over her and would knock her flat if he hadn't kept himself contained.

He'd put a dampening field around himself, she thought. If he hadn't, he might have overwhelmed her senses and either sent her flying off the mountain or doubling over with a heart attack.

"He is Dionysus," Pol said. "Do not worry. He won't hurt one of ours."

Fiona gave him a skeptical look. The god laughed, a sound that filled the valley.

"She is wise for her years. But this is a greeting of old friends, Fiona. A cup of wine, a kiss…"

Cas' arm tightened around her. "We saw her first."

Dionysus laughed again. "I know. I can't help it. Sit, Fiona. Drink wine with us and tell us your story. Something has happened."

Fiona started to ask how he knew then decided not to worry about it.

Cas sat on the cloth of gold and pulled her down to his lap. It seemed perfectly natural to sprawl across his legs and drink rich, mellow wine from a gold cup he held for her. After she drank, he licked a drop of wine from her mouth and lifted the cup to his own lips.

Pol sat close on her other side, resting his hand ever-so casually on her thigh. He unwrapped the terracotta vessel and set it on the cloth, and they all studied the painted portraits of the twins, mirror images, standing with arms folded, backs to each other.

Dionysus drained a goblet of wine and shook his head. "Selena is too full of herself. Tell us what happened, Fiona."

Fiona related the research she'd done in the library and the encounter with Selena. For some reason, she left out the part about the cat. She wanted to tell them and speculate on who the cat had been, but every time she began to speak about it, her lips and tongue felt heavy and she fell silent.

Dionysus gave her a narrow look but said nothing. *He* knew she was leaving something out, but to her relief said nothing.

When she finished, she lay against Cas' strong shoulder, his arms supporting her and his lap cradling her. He smelled so good, like the fresh grass and the air around them and his own masculine scent.

Cas growled. "I'll not leave you alone again. I did not know your magic places would be dangerous for you."

Dionysus lay on his back, one leg bent, arms behind his head, watching the clouds drift by. "I'd kill Selena," he mused. "But Poseidon would not let me. He hates her, but she is his. He's strange like that."

"We'll have to castrate her somehow," Pol said. "But if she touches you again, Fiona, I'll risk Poseidon's wrath and strangle her. It will be an ugly fight, but I'll do it."

"Be careful," Fiona said. "I don't think she's quite sane."

Dionysus snorted. "An understatement. She's been crazy as a loon since the day she was hatched. A more interesting problem is the spell on the jar." He lifted the terracotta jug and examined it closely. "You say you don't know what will happen if it breaks?"

He lifted it in his sinewy hands as though prepared to hurl it toward some rocks in the middle of the meadow.

"No!" Fiona leapt for him and closed her hands around the vessel.

She met his black-gold gaze and for a moment felt as though he sucked her right into him. She was falling into velvet darkness that caressed her body like a lover. It was the height of sensuality and at the same time absolutely terrifying.

"Leave her be," Cas rumbled behind her.

The god grinned and the darkness receded, leaving her looking at a handsome man who held out the jar to her.

She took it carefully and set it on the pillows. "They might die or might be sent back to oblivion."

"That would be a shame," Dionysus said.

"I'd say so," Pol put in.

Cas said nothing. His eyes darkened as he watched Fiona, and suddenly she wanted that erotic darkness Dionysus had made her see, but she wanted it with Cas. They could be pressed body to body, lounging on soft velvet with his cock buried high inside her, his tongue in her mouth.

She looked at him and knew he wanted it too. He wanted *her*, Fiona, not because of her expertise on pottery or the fact that she was available to crawl around digs with scorpions and rats, he wanted Fiona the woman. No other person in her life had wanted Fiona the woman.

Fiona touched his hand. He covered hers in his, his finger tracing her palm.

She saw Pol standing behind him, his eyes as intense on her. She remembered taking him far into her mouth and the smooth taste of his come. Pol wanted her too.

"Selena is a danger as long as you are alive," Dionysus was saying.

Fiona felt a surge of power from him, one her mind tried to dampen. The power flared and built until it crawled under her skin like strange electricity.

"But I'm going to give you a gift," the god went on. "A reprieve before you have to find her and face her, because face her you must."

He stepped beside the twins and put one hand on each man's shoulder. "I will give you the gift — of time."

The mountain swirled away with incredible speed, but before Fiona could cry out they were standing in soft darkness, inside the two rooms she'd rented at the tiny inn.

Chapter Nine

ℰᏅ

Cas heard music coming from somewhere down the street, a lone man singing about his beloved and the beautiful countryside. In his arms, Fiona started. She looked tired, her white face lined with exhaustion and worry.

He fumed that Selena had confronted her and tried to hurt her. Fiona was innocent—she had no idea what vindictive wrath a demigoddess could have for no reason at all. Selena would be punished for frightening her.

He ran his hand through her warm hair. His brave Fiona, standing up to a demigoddess and stealing the jar to keep it safe.

She was looking around in confusion, her pretty eyes shining in the dark. "This is where I spent the night last night. And I remember that man singing down the street. It soothed me to sleep. What happened?"

"A gift of time," Pol said. He leaned against the door, his t-shirt a pale smudge in the dark. "Dionysus is letting us have the night again, free from danger."

"He can do that? Do we have to be careful not to see our other selves or disrupt the time stream or something?"

Pol chuckled. "It isn't time travel. We live the night *over again*. As though we didn't do it the first time. We're safe here, and he's letting us enjoy it."

"Oh."

Cas smiled at Fiona's bafflement. Dionysus being who he was, Cas had a pretty good idea how the god expected them to enjoy themselves. He ran his fingers lightly down Fiona's arm.

"Fiona will need to rest. In bed."

Pol laughed out loud. Cas could see Fiona's blush even in the darkness, but her hand tightened around his.

"I leave you to your delights," Pol said, pushing himself from the doorframe. "I go in search of wine and song."

He did a slow dance step, one hand on his abdomen as he swiveled his hips. Then he laughed softly and sauntered out the door, closing it behind him.

Fiona turned to Cas, eyes wide and questioning. It took effort to not throw her down and ravish her on the spot.

"You are surprised Pol left us?" he asked.

She laid her head on his chest, a warm armful of woman. "A little."

"He knows what I want. He too is giving me a gift."

Fiona smiled suddenly and raised on tiptoe to kiss the side of his mouth. "We should not waste it then."

"No, we should not."

He kissed her deeply, then he took both her hands and led her into the bedroom.

* * * * *

Pol walked down the street smiling, imagining steam rolling from the inn he left behind. He'd never seen Cas so far gone on a woman before.

But then, *what* a woman. Red hair like fire-colored silk, eyes swimming with sensuality, even her grubby fingers were cute. A lady who liked to play in the dirt.

He stopped, enjoying a sudden vision of dirt all over her nude body as she rolled in the dust, laughing. He was surprised the other archaeologists weren't all over her. But the shortsighted people were, like Hans, so enamored of digging up the past that they couldn't see what was right in front of them in the present.

If anything, Pol should be obsessed by the past, wanting to know what he'd missed while trapped in the painting. But he'd lived for thousands of years before Selena and her sorcery, and he'd learned that the present was always the most important time to be in. Never forget the past, was his motto, but live for the here and now.

Pol walked on toward the lights and noise of the taverna. They were safe from Selena tonight, thanks to Dionysus, and he could enjoy drink and dance and a woman if he wanted her.

No, he knew which woman he wanted. Wanted to touch every part of her with every part of himself.

Fiona.

The very woman his brother was about to fuck in a frenzy of passion while Pol sat in a corner in a taverna and drank wine.

Hmm. Well, he'd give them some time. How much time? An hour? No, longer. Cas would want to savor it.

Pol would give his brother long enough to sate himself then he'd would return and see what he could convince them both to do.

The twins had shared everything in their entire existence, and Pol saw no reason to stop now.

* * * * *

"Do you like that?"

Cas stroked his hands down Fiona's naked abdomen, his palms calloused and warm. She moved her hips, both wanting him to hurry and finish stripping her and wanting him to take his time.

"Do you like it?" he asked again.

"I do. Can't you tell?"

"Your eyes give nothing away."

Cas leaned over her, still dressed, until his face was an inch from hers. His breath heated her skin, then he soothed her eyelids closed with his lips.

After Pol had departed, Cas had said not a word. No crude, "Hey, baby, want to do it?" or more romantic offers of lovemaking. He'd simply lifted her into his arms, carried her into the bedroom and laid her on the bed.

The whitewashed room contained a simple bedstead of white wood and a night table and dresser to match. Two Byzantine icons were framed over the dresser, and that was it for decoration.

Fiona loved the room's simplicity, which soothed and relaxed her. She had the feeling she'd love it even more after tonight.

Cas had proceeded to unbutton her shirt and pull it open then he'd began massaging her stomach and breasts, his touch arousing and comforting at the same time.

"I haven't been—with—anyone for a long time," she said.

"I haven't been with anyone for twenty-five hundred years. I believe I have, as you Americans say, broken your record."

She touched his face, loving the sandpaper feel of his dark whiskers. "Hope you haven't forgotten anything."

"I believe it comes naturally and time between does not matter."

"Like riding a bicycle," she suggested.

Cas frowned. "*Bicycle*?"

"Like the motorcycle. Only without a motor."

"Ah, I saw those. How foolish to force yourself to pedal when your magic motors can propel you very fast."

Fiona remembered the descriptions villagers had given her of Cas driving the motorcycle through small villages. They'd not said he'd driven *fast*. The term *maniac* had cropped up most often.

She thought she probably should explain a few traffic rules to him, but at that moment he unhooked her bra and slid it gently from her body, and she lost her train of thought.

Cas ran his thumbs across her breasts, stroking her nipples into tight peaks before leaning down and taking one in his mouth.

"You don't have to ask whether I like that," she gasped. "I do."

"I know." He kissed her skin then drew the tip of his tongue slowly between her breasts.

"My body tells you more than my eyes, then."

Cas focused flatteringly on her torso, letting his gaze drift to her throat. "It tells me much. It tells me you want me to touch it."

"*Please.*"

The only light in the room came from a lone candle on the dresser and the moonlight without. Beyond the window, over the rooftops of the tiny village, the dark bulk of Mount Olympus hovered.

The domain of the gods. She believed that now.

She had many questions about Dionysus and what he really looked like and how he'd gotten her from the lower slopes to nearly the top without her noticing. But questions could wait, she decided, drifting into hazy pleasure as Cas unzipped her very practical cotton shorts.

He eased the shorts over her legs and feet, then he unlaced her sneakers and stripped off her socks. He stroked his hands down her thighs and behind her calves before warming the soles of her feet.

Then he leaned down and nibbled her toes. Fiona rolled her hips, digging into the bed. His mouth was warm and wet and very erotic.

He pressed a long kiss to the instep of her right foot, then skimmed his hands back up her legs to her underwear, which he proceeded to strip from her.

"So now you have me naked," Fiona said, her skin prickling under his appreciative gaze. "Why are you still dressed?"

"I am enjoying watching you and making you want me. I want you to want me so much you scream for me."

Warmth pooled in her belly and she felt the slide of cream on her thighs. "I'm thinking it won't take much before I'm screaming."

He smiled and stroked his palm across her quim. She jumped, biting back a sharp cry.

"I like this idea." He stroked her again, and again her hips rose, needing his hand to press there.

Fiona's legs opened of their own accord, her quim wet and wanting him. She put her hand to it, like he'd dared her to last night, and stirred the folds with her fingers.

"I will fuck you, my Fiona. But when I am ready."

She pressed her hand to the rigid bulge in his jeans. "You mean you're not ready now?"

He laughed softly. "Yes, but it is amusing to tease you."

Fiona hooked her finger over his belt buckle. "Get those pants off and get down here, mister."

"What is this *mister*? Is it a name for a lover?"

"The name of my lover is *Cas*."

He gave her a slow smile as though he'd been waiting all day for her to say so.

Where this sexy, bantering woman had come from, Fiona had no idea. She certainly didn't recognize her. Maybe Dionysus had given her a gift of boldness along with the gift of time.

Or maybe Cas was just too damn sexy to resist. He kept slanting her glances of pure sin as he slipped his belt through the buckle and slid it from his jeans.

He stripped off his t-shirt and let it fall, giving her a fantastic view of his tight abdomen encased in bronze skin. She liked his navel, a smooth indentation above his pelvis.

He shouldn't have a navel, it suddenly struck her, because Castor and Pollux had been hatched from eggs, after Zeus — in the form of a swan — had seduced Leda. But then, mythology didn't have to make sense.

The point was that Zeus and Leda had created this beautiful man called Cas and his brother Pol. Helen of Troy had been their sister. If Cas and Pol were anything to go by, no wonder the woman's beauty had caused the destruction of a nation.

Cas unbuttoned and unzipped his jeans and let them drop. Like Pol the night before, Cas wore nothing underneath.

"Why does the no-underwear thing turn me on so much?" she wondered.

"Does it?" He looked pleased. "I did not know I was supposed to wear it."

"Oh." That made sense—Cas and Pol had lifted things from Hans' wardrobe to cover their legs and torsos. Why would they think to go rooting in Hans' underwear drawer?

She was glad Cas was a demigod and didn't have a clue what underwear was. All the faster to get him naked. She rolled onto her side and did what she'd been longing to do since she met him—she closed her mouth over his cock.

"Mmm." Cas laced his fingers through her hair, but gently, unlike Pol, who'd dragged her against him.

He tasted different from Pol. Pol had been spicy, a little like pepper. Cas was smooth and mellow, a strong, heady delight. She ran her tongue around his flange, tasting every inch of him while he threaded his fingers through her hair.

She drew back slowly, holding the weight of him on her tongue until the very last minute.

"Can we?" she whispered. "Please?"

His eyes were pools of midnight. "Yes." He pressed her back to the bed and climbed over her, knees on either side of her. "I need you."

Fiona lifted her hips, fire running to every fingertip. His warm weight was so *satisfying*, his limbs strong and fine, fitting against her in perfect accord. He nudged her thighs apart and rested his firm tip against her opening.

She cupped his buttocks, wanting him in, but he hovered there, letting her quim grow more and more open and wet and needy. She dug her fingers into his skin. "Please, Cas."

He braced himself, holding back. "Have you ever been with a demigod, Fiona?"

She gasped, trying not to laugh. "I can safely say I haven't."

"It isn't the same as being with a human. You will have all of me, and I all of you."

"Sounds good to me."

"You do not understand."

"No, but I want to."

He gave her a look that said *I warned you* and slid his cock halfway into her.

Fiona's eyes widened. Cas was right, she *didn't* understand, and myriad sensations hit her at once. First was the feel of his enormous cock stretching her wide to admit him, her walls closing around him and squeezing him.

Next was the feel of his satin-warm skin on hers, his weight pressing her into the yielding mattress, his heat covering her entire body. She felt his legs stretched the length of hers, his wiry black hair rough against her thighs.

She also felt *her* around *him*. His body seemed to blur, like Dionysus' had, the god half of Cas shimmering into focus and out of it. Tendrils of feeling laced her mind, hot excitement, the sensation of squeezing.

She realized that the feelings were not hers, but his. His mind and hers were locked, and she saw what he saw, felt what he felt. She could see herself beneath him, her face twisting in passion, and experience the sensation of her quim pulsing around his cock.

She also felt him inside her, sliding and rubbing and driving her crazy. She couldn't shake him out of her, and she realized that he felt everything she did. *You will have all of me, and I all of you.*

After her first panicked moment, an ecstasy unlike anything she'd felt in her life poured over her. She screamed and he kissed her, smothering her cries. She dug her fingers into his backside and tried to pull him farther into her.

He hesitated for a maddening moment then he slid all the way in. He groaned against her lips and she experienced his sudden elation at feeling her surrounding every inch of him.

Every inch of him was right. Cas was huge, and he was in all the way to his balls.

"Fiona," he whispered, voice hoarse. "You are so tight, you feel so good."

She experienced the tightness with him. She felt both the pressure of herself on him and the pressure of him stretching her wide, impossibly wide.

Double ecstasy, double pleasure, oh gods, she couldn't stand it.

He moved out again, almost to his tip and slid back in, hard, his eyes widening in the dark.

Moonlight played on his muscles as he held himself in her, not moving, giving her a chance to get used to him. Her legs were stretched open, knees on either side of the narrow bed, her hips lifted to let him fill her.

She felt their hearts racing while they waited. His eyes held something raw and dark, a need beyond sex.

He was a man out of time and he needed to belong somewhere. He thought that maybe, just maybe, he belonged with her.

Yes, Fiona thought, wondering if she were reading his mind. *Stay here with me.*

He growled deep in his throat, his control vanishing. His brows drawing into a fearsome scowl, he thrust hard into her, quickly and remorselessly. He began to pump her, widening her legs with each thrust.

Fiona realized what he meant when he'd said she needed to be ready for him. He was big and he was strong and he was not going to be gentle.

He couldn't, not now. Later, maybe, he'd show her good, slow loving, but right now he was desperate and lonely — twenty-five hundred years worth of lonely.

She felt that loneliness pour through him, his muscles tight beneath her fingers, his blood thrumming. She felt the intense pressure of herself squeezing him and his need to drive farther and farther into her. He needed her, needed to be home, and home was in her arms.

At least, that's what his body told her. She felt everything he did, and felt him sliding inside her, his cock huge and hard and unmerciful.

She forgot all about containing her cries and worrying about who might hear. She lolled her head back on the pillow and groaned, raising her hips to take more of him.

His thrusts crushed her buttocks into the thin mattress, her thighs aching where they spread. He hurt her and he made her feel fiery hot and so damn good she had to scream.

She'd never had a fucking like this. Whatever she'd done before hadn't really been *fucking*, not in this raw, aching, beautiful sense. A few thrusts in and out before she could really feel them, that had been it.

She felt all of Cas, saw the intensity of his eyes when he caught her gaze and refused to release it. The raw sounds in his throat only made the hot feel of him between her legs better.

He was feeling it and loving it and wasn't about to stop.

Their joined senses made the pressure in her quim even more powerful. She felt herself pulse around his cock, felt the joy of that burning. She screamed with it, wondering how the hell he contained himself.

An orgasm rocked her, the first one she'd ever had while penetrated. Cas' dark gaze grew even more feral and he reached one finger between their bodies to rub her clit.

She got lost in mindless darkness. She had no idea where she was. She only knew she lay on a hard slab of bed and that Cas drove in and out of her so hard she thought she'd die.

She'd go with a smile on her face, that was for certain. Fiona McCarty, promising young archaeologist, passing away while being fucked by a muscular, beautiful man she'd rescued from a painting on a jar.

She laughed with joy. Cas growled, pressing her into the bed until she came again.

Still he went on, his cock so hard he could have pounded nails with it. She felt the buildup inside him, the pulsing behind his balls that meant he wanted to come, the incredible will with which he held himself back until the last possible minute.

When he exploded inside her, she thought she saw the ceiling rip away and the stars of the night cascade down on them. She writhed her hips against his, crying with the pure joy of it. Her shouts mingled with his as they came together, their voices twining into the silence of the night.

Chapter Ten

** so**

Fiona lay quietly with Cas for a long time. Her body still hummed with heat and their fierce lovemaking, but she was also content to lie with him as they touched and kissed.

His kisses were so gentle, she couldn't believe he was the same demigod who had given her sex so raw she wasn't sure she could walk again.

He played with her a little, bringing her to readiness, then entered her again, slow, quiet and strong, his dark gaze locking hers. It went on for a long, long time, slowly building her to a frenzy, taking her down before she climaxed and building her up again.

At last he let her come. She screamed and writhed and he kissed her hard, dragging her cries into his mouth. He slowed after that, then withdrew from her and closed his eyes.

After that he fell into a profound sleep, with Fiona watching him, relaxed and happy but not tired.

She started to feel restless, so she left the bedroom for the darkness of the front room. She ruffled her hair to soak up the cool breeze from the window and glanced back at Cas.

He lay sprawled across the bed, naked and snoring, cradling his head on one arm. Moonlight brushed his skin and glistened on his very black hair and touched the curls at his cock, which lay half deflated, but no less large.

Fiona smiled as she closed the door and let him sleep. In her sexual encounters of the past, she'd usually collapsed with tiredness and disappointment. This time she felt blissfully happy and energized enough to jog around the block.

She could take a walk, she supposed. As with everywhere else in Greece, people in this village stayed up far into the night, and her walking around would not be unusual.

She pulled a shirt over her nakedness but was in no hurry. She went to the open window and rested her arms on the sill, looking down at the whitewashed village under the stars. The music at the taverna still played, stringed notes vibrating into the night.

After a moment, she realized Pol was down on the street looking up at her. How long he'd been standing there, she couldn't tell, but there was a knowing smile on his face.

When he caught her gaze, he gave her a slow nod and sauntered to the inn's door and came inside.

Fiona remained at the window, absorbing the stars and the breeze and the music, reflecting that for the first time in her life, she was happy. Or as happy as she could be wondering which of a pair of twins she was falling in love with, and whether, because they were demigods and pretty much immortal, they could ever possibly love her back.

Then she had to figure out how to make sure Selena didn't trap them again and how to break the spell that bound them to the jar. All in a day's work for Indiana Jones, but not for plain Fiona McCarty, pottery specialist from the University of Chicago.

She heard Pol's footsteps on the narrow staircase and then he opened the door. For some reason, she still did not turn as he shut the door and walked softly to her. She closely her eyes briefly as he stopped behind her and leaned his hands on the windowsill, enclosing her with his warm body.

"Have a good sleep?" He kissed her hair. "Or did my brother manage to keep you awake?"

Fiona shivered, remembering her last wild orgasm and the dual experience of Cas' orgasm as they came together.

"That good, eh?" Pol kissed her hair again, lips drifting to the skin at her temple. "He outdid himself."

"It was the best I ever had," Fiona said softly.

Pol drew his tongue along the shell of her ear, and even sated as she was, the juices between her thighs began to flow.

"A challenge," Pol murmured. "Are you up for it?"

She really shouldn't. Cas, the man she loved, lay in bed, naked and sexy. She should return and snuggle up with him and tell Pol to find someone else at the taverna.

But then Pol, the other man she loved, was close behind her, *dressed* and sexy, his warmth swallowing her.

"I think I'm up for it," she found herself saying.

"Gooood." He drew out the word. She felt fingers ease under her shirt to her buttocks. "Bare, just how I like you."

She started to turn around, but he nipped her ear. "Stay where you are."

The little growl in his voice made her pulse speed. She remembered how he'd ordered her to strip in the pottery room and how she'd so eagerly done it. She wondered if he'd sent his feelings into her head as Cas had done, making her behave like a tart because he wanted her to.

It didn't really matter, because she'd do it again in a heartbeat.

His warm finger dipped between her buttocks, massaging and rubbing. "Have you ever had a man here?"

Fiona rocked forward on the windowsill, excitement building inside her until her legs shook. "No. And not a demigod, either."

Pol laughed out loud, then softened the laugh. "So Cas didn't explore yet. I told him I'd let him fuck you first, but I didn't say where *I* wanted to fuck you."

"Where do you?"

"Where do I what?"

Fiona swallowed, feeling his breath on her neck, his black hair sliding on the collar of her shirt, the warmth of his body against hers, and the exciting point of his fingertip finding and stroking her anal star.

"Where do I what?" he repeated, voice stronger. "Say it, sweetheart."

"Where do you want to fuck me?" she whispered.

"I could not hear you, love. Say it out loud."

Fiona groaned, excitement mounting as his finger dipped the slightest bit into her ass. "Where do you want to fuck me?"

"I think you can guess."

He drew his tongue up the side of her neck as he slowly but firmly pressed his finger farther into her. She was so damn wet, cream slicking her skin and pooling inside her pussy, wanting him so much.

"I can't take it," she gasped.

"Yes, you can."

Pol slowly eased his body away from her then withdrew his finger from her ass a fraction of an inch at a time.

When he finally released her, Fiona turned around and leaned against the windowsill, hugging her chest. She breathed hard, her throat dry and tight. "I don't know if I can."

Pol's eyes were dark as sin, his smile nearly taking her to the point of orgasm without him even touching her. "You can. I have the patience to teach you. All you have to do is surrender yourself absolutely to me."

She gave a shaky laugh. "That's all, is it?"

Pol came close to her and brushed a lock of hair from her forehead. "If you don't surrender yourself, I might hurt you. You have to be relaxed and open to take me, and you can only do that if you let me have full control over you."

"Full control. Oh my."

She thought she'd adore being under his full control, doing anything he said and reaping the incredible feelings he would give her. If he made love anything like Cas did, she was in for a rare treat.

Her years of training as a scholar, of not accepting everything at face value and not getting excited until something was verified, made her hesitate a little. Giving up control was something Fiona was very bad at.

But Pol was right. She'd *read* about what he wanted to do, although she'd never done it herself or dreamed any man would offer. If the woman wasn't completely relaxed and trusting, it could be painful.

On the other hand, if the woman surrendered her body to her lover, the results could be astonishing.

Before her hesitant self could interfere, Fiona said, "I'll do it."

He grinned in the dark, folding his arms over his broad chest. "Then turn around and bend yourself across that table."

He nodded toward the bare wooden table to one side of the room, surrounded by gaily painted wooden chairs.

Fiona studied it, a simple piece of furniture about to be transformed into an erotic jungle gym.

Slowly she approached it, moved a chair out of the way and leaned over, stretching her torso and arms across the cool, hard surface.

"Will it be too high?" she asked. Her legs and body made a perfect right angle, and she had the idea that her butt had to be elevated.

"'Twill be fine."

She heard him approach then felt something at her feet. "Stand on this," he said.

She looked down and saw a painted wooden stepstool, longer than it was wide, resting where Pol had set it. Obediently, she stepped up on it and bent over again.

Pol rested his hands on her hips. "Perfect." He slid her shirt upward, baring her ass, rubbing her hips and buttocks briskly until they warmed. "Are you ready, love?"

Fiona gulped, her unfettered breasts pressing into the table. "Won't Cas wake up?"

"Cas could sleep through a Bacchanalia. I know this for a fact, I've watched him do it. He missed *all* the fun *that* night." He leaned over her, the ridge of his jeans-encased cock pressing the length of her crease. "Are you ready?"

Fiona gulped. "Sure. Why not?"

To her complete disappointment, he backed away. She turned her head to watch him move to a shadow on the floor near the door. "I happened to purchase a bottle of fine oil while I was out. Lavender, I think it is."

"You *happened* to purchase it?" Fiona asked.

"I *wonder* why I decided to do that?"

His voice was full of smiles. He came back to her and set a glass bottle next to her where she could see it. Pol worked out the glass stopper with sinewy fingers and laid it on the table. The sweet scent of lavender floated to her.

Pol lifted the bottle and poured a stream of glistening oil over his fingers. He leaned close to Fiona as he set down the bottle and stoppered it. "Now, Fiona. Give yourself to me."

He rested the hand he hadn't oiled on her head, the weight warm. Fiona drew a breath and slowly let it out, willing her body to relax.

A warmth shot through her, followed by the sensation of fire. She gasped and tensed, then let out her breath again as she realized that Pol had connected with her, just as Cas had done.

She could feel her hair against Pol's palm, could feel the sleek oil that coated his fingers with the same intensity that she felt the table beneath her and her bare feet on the stool. The hammering of her heart matched his.

When he parted her buttocks again, she felt his fingers on her as well as the firm tightness of her anal star. She groaned as he slid one slick finger inside her.

It was as though she pleasured herself at the same time he pleasured her. She felt every inch of herself around his finger, every flex of his finger inside her. She squeezed and relaxed, not even aware she did it.

"That is good," Pol said softly. "Exactly like that. Do it again."

She tried to get her body to obey, but only when she let go of the control did she squeeze hard and release, opening more each time.

"Perfect." Pol's voice soothed her. "You need to be ready for me. I'm big, sweetheart."

Fiona knew that already. She'd held his lovely cock in her hand and taken it in her mouth, and the thought that she'd soon have it in her ass sent her spiraling toward climax.

Pol laughed, feeling her excitement. "You're moving too fast. Wait for me."

Fiona opened her mouth to laugh with him, then she let out a tiny scream as a second finger joined his first. "Oh gods."

"How do you feel, love?" He leaned over, careful not to move his fingers too fast, and brushed a kiss to her cheek.

"Full," she said. "Full and tight...and open."

"Good. That's how I want you to feel. Keep taking me, love." He moved his fingers in and out, slowly, in perfect rhythm. Fiona felt herself relax, wanting his fingers deeper with every push, wanted to open and accept more of him.

"Oh, sweetheart, you are *good* at this."

Pol's approval made her shiver in delight. She felt so wanton and so excited at the same time, bent over the table, the cool wood against her cheek, with her ass in the air and a gorgeous man's fingers sliding in and out of her. She was wicked and sexy, and she loved it.

Pol withdrew and replenished the oil on his fingers. The bottle clunked back to the table, then she squealed in delight when he slid *three* fingers into her.

"Ooohhhh," she moaned, moving quickly toward incoherence. Her hips moved of their own accord, she babbled meaningless sounds, and above all she *loved* what he did to her.

The beautiful thing was, if he liked it, she could do the same to him, give him this same pleasure she was enjoying the heck out of.

But there was one pleasure she couldn't give him. After a nice ten minutes of him playing with her with his three fingers he withdrew his hand and reached for the bottle of oil.

Then at her opening she felt the firm bluntness of his cock, slick with oil.

"Oh, Pol," she begged. "Please."

He positioned himself at her anal star, which had relaxed and widened until Fiona was weak in the knees. Only the table kept her from falling over completely, and her hips rose in anticipation.

"Slowly. I'll do it slowly. I don't want to hurt you."

"Please, Pol, make it hurt good."

He chuckled. "Darling, you are a demigod's dream come true."

Carefully, almost unbearably so, Pol pushed the tip of his cock inside her.

"It's good," she panted. "It's good, it's *so* good."

"It is." Pol's voice was a groan. "Fiona, you are so fucking tight."

"More. I want more."

"When you're ready, sweetheart. Oh gods."

His voice broke as more of his oiled cock slipped inside her. He gripped the edges of the table—she sensed his hands biting into the wood as the feeling of her squeezing him rampaged him.

Slowly, just as slowly as Cas had pushed himself into her pussy, Pol slid himself into her ass.

He took his time. She felt the pulse that raced through his cock against her walls, spreading her, relaxing her, transferring his excitement to her.

She'd never felt anything like it in her life. It burned and hurt and at the same time she was so open and accepting.

She groaned into the tabletop, her voice echoing from the wood. Pol pressed himself deep inside, the feral sounds he made exciting her.

"I know why my brother loves you," he whispered, voice ragged. "I know why he thinks you're sweet."

"I love him," she moaned.

"I know, baby. I know. You feel so good."

His cock moved. He began to slowly withdraw then he pressed back in, his hands hard on the tabletop.

As with Cas, she felt what he felt, the silken ends of his own hair brushing his shoulders as he threw back his head, the firm press of her on the length of his cock, the buildup inside him.

Her first orgasm hit her swiftly, before she even knew it was coming. She writhed against the table, the edge rubbing her pussy in a satisfying way. "Fuck me," she cried.

"Most definitely."

Pol moved smoothly in and out, holding himself hard to keep the pain at bay, to make sure she felt only pleasure.

Fiona's heart pumped with joy and gratitude. Pol was a demigod. He could play with her and hurt her and discard her — mythology was filled with gods, demigods and heroes who weren't exactly kind to the women they seduced.

But like Cas, he was taking it slow when he didn't have to, giving her pleasure when he didn't have to.

He could take what he wanted and not care what she felt. He was far more powerful than she and he knew it.

But she trusted him. If he had been Dionysus, the god whose terrible power she'd glimpsed earlier that day, she'd be terrified. But this was Pol of the wicked smiles and dark eyes and hands that caressed and soothed her.

Both Pol and Cas had made sure she was ready to take a demigod.

She felt more than ready. "Please, Pol," she gasped. "More, *please*."

Pol laughed, his voice hoarse. "If you insist."

The moment her orgasm died off, another swelled in its place. She felt his impending orgasm at the same time, his excitement at being pushed into her as far as he could go.

"Thank you," he groaned. "Fiona, you're so fucking good."

"I can't stand it."

"Yes you can, baby. Just a little longer."

She squealed and moaned against the table, the wood cool on her face. Her entire body was hot, her limbs heavy, but at the same time she was wound tight with excitement.

How many times could she orgasm tonight? The way Pol laughed behind her he intended her to do it several times more.

And then—"No," he gasped. "Not yet."

Fiona wriggled against him, wanting him to come as much as she wanted this incredible feeling to go on forever.

His seed shot inside her as he crushed her hips against him. The spinning darkness in his mind crashed over her along with her own emotions, a double orgasm—filling them both.

They both breathed hard and raw as Pol slid out of her and leaned over her on the table. She felt every inch of his hard-muscled body melding into her back and thighs, his limbs heavy with release.

A surge of satisfaction welled through her. He'd stretched her so wide, and yet she could do it, she could take him.

They stayed like that for a long time, both knowing they needed to wind down, neither wanting to.

Pol pressed kisses to her hair, nuzzling her. "You are good at that, sweetheart. You've never done it before?"

"No. I'm sure I'd remember *that*."

"Thank you for letting me be the first."

She grinned against the tabletop. "My pleasure."

Pol straightened, taking away his warm weight. Fiona's heart squeezed in disappointment. She wanted him, like Cas, to take her into his arms and touch her a little longer.

Pol patted her backside. She heard him slip on his jeans and zip them up then slide the sandals back on his feet.

"I think I need a walk after that. Come with me to the taverna?"

Fiona groaned. If she went to a taverna and drank wine right now, she'd slither right under the table. Pol would have to carry her home over his shoulder, and then they might get up to more fun.

She groaned again. "No, I need to sleep."

He laughed softly as though knowing exactly why she couldn't move. "Go and snuggle with Cas. He'll like that."

He gave her ass another pat then walked out the door.

She stayed bent over the table, unable to make her limbs move as she heard him move down the stairs and back to the street. She could fall asleep here, her butt in the air, her cheek pressed against the cool wood. Wouldn't that look ridiculous when the maid came in tomorrow?

But it was a nice table, very comfortable. Her legs were nearly numb, but that was fine. If she fell she doubted she'd feel a thing.

Who knew she could stand so much sex, and who knew she'd love it like this? She'd never realized there was a wild, wicked, *fun* Fiona inside her who thought nothing of having missionary-position sex with one man and then having anal sex with his brother in the next room.

And the missionary-position sex—the usual way a man and woman made love in the dark—had been nothing short of mind-blowing. She'd have plain old sex like that any day of the week. And on weekends and holidays too.

She heard Pol walk by outside, his step light, whistling. How he could be so energetic after fucking her like that, she didn't know. She thought she'd sleep for a week.

Speaking of which, she really couldn't fall asleep on the table. Her body thought about the soft nest in the bedroom with Cas already in it and wanted to go there.

She finally straightened up, moving gingerly, and stepped off the stool. She yawned and stretched then turned to the bedroom door.

She froze, heart in her throat. Cas was leaning on the doorframe of the open door to the bedroom, his arms folded across his bare chest, his brows drawn into a fearsome scowl.

Chapter Eleven

ဆာ

He wore nothing but his jeans, the waistband riding low on his hips, moonlight playing on his bare torso. His intense gaze held hers, eyes glittering in the dark.

Fiona gulped. "Cas."

He remained fixed, his body shadowed. He was the beautifully wrought statue of a demigod, only his hair stirring in the faint breeze from the window.

Fiona's shirt had slid down to cover her bare ass, but she felt more exposed than she ever had in her life. "You saw," she whispered.

Cas didn't answer. He watched her, his face set, his body utterly still.

Fiona's heart raced. She loved Cas. She wanted *him* to love her, and the thought of hurting him broke her heart. And yet Pol…

"Get on the table," Cas said. "On your back."

She blinked at him. "What?"

"*Now.*"

The word was harsh and didn't want to take no for an answer. Fiona retreated to the table, and under his unwavering gaze, stepped up on the stepstool and sat her butt on the edge of the table.

"Lie down," he commanded.

Fiona slowly lay back, the tabletop hard against her spine. She breathed rapidly and wondered how much more of Cas and Pol she could take tonight.

Cas remained by the door. "Pull up your shirt. Show me your pussy."

Well, maybe she could take a *little* more. She lifted the hem of the long shirt and spread her thighs a little.

"Show it to me," Cas said. He pushed himself from the doorframe and moved toward her slowly, like a panther stalking its prey. "Show me how wet it is."

Fiona tentatively moved her fingers through her folds, drawing a fingertip across the opening of her quim. Cream obligingly flowed out to cover her fingers.

Cas made a noise in his throat. He stopped at the end of the table, standing as motionlessly as a big cat, his eyes as glittering as a predator's. He slid the stool out of the way and stood between Fiona's legs, his dark gaze taking in her rumpled shirt, her body spread before him, her fingers playing in her quim.

He watched for a moment longer, then swiftly unzipped his jeans and let them rest on his thighs, not bothering to kick them off. He grasped her ankles with firm hands and jerked them to his shoulders, lifting her hips from the table.

His face set, he positioned his cock on her opening and shoved it inside.

There was no waiting until she got used to him or until their feelings melded. He began to take her with hard thrusts, one, two, three... Moving faster and faster. Her back banged against the table, which rocked and creaked under the onslaught.

He held her legs firmly and fucked her hard as the table legs groaned against the floor. *Fucking* was the right word. This was no lovemaking. He'd seen what Pol had done to her and he was punishing her.

Punishing her by driving his cock into her. She lifted her hips, meeting his thrusts, squirming and eager. She felt him and herself at the same time, smelled the scent of her cream and his cock and Pol's come, a fine cocktail for her nose.

He pounded into her, hips crashing against hers. He made no noise save for a few soft grunts.

"Fuck," Fiona groaned. "Fuck me, Cas. Damn, I love you so much."

He growled something unintelligible, then he closed his eyes and came. His sleek hair tickled her feet as he moved his head from side to side, hips pulsing with his climax. She rode it with him, her climax squeezing her entire body until she heard someone screaming.

The screams must have come from her, because her throat went raw and the noises became hoarse and broken.

Cas slammed into her one more time, holding himself against her hard while she squeezed him. Then he withdrew in a swift move and lifted her against him.

His arms crushed the breath out of her. He was shaking all over, his body shining with sweat, his hair damp with it. His cock lay heavy against her thigh, half rigid, indicating it could flare to life in no time at all.

Fiona twined her arms softly around his shoulders and kissed his cheek. "Cas? Are you all right? I'm sorry about Pol. I couldn't help myself. I've never done that before."

Cas hauled her upright, their faces even.

"I loved it," he said fiercely. "I loved watching him fuck you. I loved watching him make you scream."

Her eyes widened and hope flared in her heart. "You did?"

"I loved every second of it. I came, watching you. Gods, when the three of us fuck together, we'll move the world."

Pol's voice came from the doorway. "Good."

He stood there with his arms folded, his stance similar to what Cas' had been, except he was fully dressed and smelled of a smoky taverna. "I'm glad to hear that's all settled. Can we go to bed now?"

* * * * *

They didn't actually have sex in the bedroom. By tacit agreement, Cas and Pol lay on either side of Fiona, as they had the first night they'd seen her, enclosing her with their protective bodies, and let her sleep.

Cas inhaled her scent as he ran his hand over her bare hip. This had been the best night of his demigod life—taking Fiona completely on the bed, watching Pol play with her and fuck her ass while he stood noiselessly in the bedroom doorway, and then fucking her hard and fast on the table, his need primal.

Pol lay on Fiona's other side, eyes closed, a happy smile on his face. Cas wondered if Pol had the same depth of feeling for Fiona that he had, or whether his brother was simply enjoying himself.

He hoped Pol loved Fiona as much as he did. Their life in this new world would be so much better if they were all together, a threesome bound by love.

Not to mention excellent sex.

Cas wanted to have Fiona in every way possible, and he wanted Pol to try things with her while he watched. Endless possibilities danced through his mind.

Fiona was a mortal woman, however, and they needed to go carefully. She was tired and needed her rest.

He'd realized after making love to her that she was not a goddess or demigoddess as he'd assumed, but a human woman fortified only with the magic of her archaeology. He had little doubt she'd come up with a way to free them of Selena and her spells completely, and then they'd have some fun.

Pol was already asleep, softly snoring, and Fiona had slid into sleep as soon as Cas pulled the sheet over her. Cas lay awake for a long time, touching Fiona and breathing in her scent, enjoying her warmth and his new feelings of love.

In the morning, Fiona announced that they needed to return to the dig. She'd taken the jar without permission, Dionysus' gift of an extra night was over and they would be safer back at the site.

Cas knew Fiona didn't really believe they'd be safer. She wore a worried pucker between her brows as she dressed, packed her toothbrush and made ready to leave.

Fiona drove her car with the jar on the seat next to her, and Cas and Pol followed on the bike. Fiona drove more slowly than Cas liked, but he did not want to venture too far ahead and leave her unprotected.

They took seven hours to reach Athens, stopping along the way to see the friends Cas and Pol had made on the way to the mountain. The families welcomed Fiona with enthusiasm and plied her with food and drink.

When they reached the site later that evening, Dr. Wheelan emerged and climbed toward them on the path.

He waved cheerfully as though they'd only been gone a few minutes instead of two entire days. "Is that the jar, Fiona? Good, I was looking for it. I have a woman here from the Greek antiquities department who wants to take it for their collection."

* * * * *

"Here?" Fiona had the sudden urge to clasp the jar to her chest and not let anyone see it. "Who is she?"

Dr. Wheelan shrugged. "A Selena something-or-other. She seems to know what she's talking about. She's waiting in the pottery room now."

Cold fear touched her. She glanced nervously at the path to the pottery room and then at the twins, who'd moved off to find Hans.

Even Dr. Wheelan would not believe that a woman dressed in black leather carrying a whip was from the antiquities department, would he? Not that Dr. Wheelan was good at noticing anything dated more recently than Roman times.

"What does she look like?"

"I don't remember. Greek. Why don't you go chat with her, Fiona, I have some…" Dr. Wheelan's words trailed off as he wandered away, his mind firmly on his next problem.

Fiona hugged the jar wrapped in its protective sheet, wanting to hide it in her room and at the same time not let it out of her sight. If she stashed it in her bedroom, what would keep Selena from sneaking in and taking it?

But then, Fiona couldn't carry it around for the rest of her life.

Exasperated, Fiona went after the twins. When she caught up to them Cas was complimenting Hans on his motorcycle and talking about how it handled. He and Hans and Pol started in on ways to ride it to make it run better, adding hand gestures to illustrate.

Men. Fiona rolled her eyes and waited until Cas looked over and saw her.

"Fiona. Love." He slid his arm around her waist and suddenly all her problems went away. At least, she wished they would. She could spend days alone in bed with this man.

Behind him Pol sent her a wink. She could spend days in bed with him as well. Or perhaps a week with both of them?

I'm in a threesome, she thought, wanting to laugh hysterically. *The woman who never believed* any *man would ever want her is in a threesome with two hot demigods.*

Hans, like Dr. Wheelan, didn't seem to notice the sudden rise in pheromones around him.

"Ah, Fiona," he said. "We are uncovering some interesting pottery fragments. Something nice for you, I think?"

"Terrific," she answered, trying to sound enthusiastic.

Fiona would normally be ecstatic at the thought of poring over totally new pottery fragments from who-knew-when. She lived for pottery. Today, however, she could barely nod and ask Hans to let her know when he had pieces ready.

As soon as they left Hans to his *stoa* Cas and Pol closed in on either side of her.

"I think Fiona should rest," Pol suggested, surreptitiously moving his fingers to her backside.

"A good idea," Cas agreed. He sent Fiona a smile that heated her blood.

"I have the feeling that if I lie down with you two I won't get much rest."

"We might let you," Pol said. "But not at first."

Her excitement grew, distracting her from the problem of Selena as she visualized what they might do. Pol would be naked on one side of her, Cas on the other, while they touched her and licked her and told her what they would do to her.

She blew out her breath, her hold nearly slipping on the jar. "Selena is here," she announced.

Both men stopped, their smiles disappearing.

"Here?" Cas' voice went hard.

"I think so. Dr. Wheelan said someone named Selena was in the pottery room."

Cas and Pol exchanged a long glance. As one, they turned and started off in the direction of the pottery room. Fiona scuttled along behind them. "Wait! If it is her, you shouldn't just run in. Let's come up with a plan for dealing with her."

"I have a plan," Pol said over his shoulder.

"What, throttle her?"

"Peel her skin from her inch by inch. *Then* throttle her."

Fiona ground her teeth. "She's very strong. I felt her power. She put the spell on you in the first place, didn't she?"

Cas faced her. "She tricked us. She used a hydra to capture Pol and threatened to murder him. She knew damn well I would not stand by and watch my brother be killed."

"You should have," Pol said.

Cas glared at him as though this was an old argument. "She said if I fucked her she'd let Pol go. I loathed her, but it seemed an easy price. I could hold my nose and do it. What I didn't know is that she could trap a man's cock in her quim."

"She paralyzed Cas," Pol filled in. "And then gave me the same choice. If I fucked her, completing the threesome, she'd let him go. But it was a ritual performed to trap us both forever."

Fiona looked from one to the other, her anger boiling up to take over reason. "Pol is right. You should throttle her."

"Damn straight," Pol answered.

They turned and strode for the pottery room.

"Carefully!" Fiona shouted after them.

She ran to catch up, heart in her throat, just as they passed into the building and crossed the threshold of the pottery room.

No one was in it. The shelves and shelves of pottery pieces were undisturbed, and they found no demon demigoddess hiding behind the door or in the shadows. If Selena had been there, she was long gone.

"It was her," Cas growled. "I can smell her."

Pol nodded, his expression grim.

Fiona loosened her hold on the jar and gently rested it on the table. "Good thing I brought this with me."

The gray tabby jumped up to the table, orange eyes bright. It sat down and yawned, its gums drawing back to reveal long, sharp teeth. Then it twined itself around the jar, butting it and purring softly.

Fiona reached her hand out to pet it.

Cas and Pol did not seem to notice. "Bring the jar, Fiona," Cas said in his quiet voice. "We will return with it to your bedchamber."

Fiona looked at the cat, who returned the look steadily. Then to her astonishment, the cat winked.

"I think I can leave it here. It will be safe for now."

Cas and Pol looked dubious. They exchanged a glance but didn't argue. The cat curled its body around the jar and proceeded to fall asleep.

＊ ＊ ＊ ＊ ＊

Cas knew it would be useless to argue with Fiona about the jar. He also knew that he and Pol would take care of it later. For now, Fiona truly needed to rest. She'd driven the little vehicle for a long time, and she'd cursed at it a lot. Sleep would do her good.

He knew, however, when they reached her small bedroom, that Fiona would not sleep, at least not right away. Pheromones poured from her, he could taste them.

Still, she calmly laid herself on the bed, promising to get some rest. Cas and Pol meant to leave but both of them stood at the foot of the bed, looking down at their lovely lady.

Perhaps he should tease her, Cas thought, driving her anticipation to the breaking point before he let her sleep. He and Pol could massage her or simply touch her and then when she was ready to be brought to climax, leave her. They could make her beg for them to return and give her release.

Of course, by then it might be himself begging for release.

He drew his hand across the soft skin of her ankle. "Which of us do you want first?"

She lifted her head, eyes widening, pupils spreading to swallow the brown. "First?"

"Your choice, love. Would you want me to make love to you slowly or do you want Pol to tie you to the bed and fuck your ass?"

Her eyes grew enormous. "I don't think I can make a choice like that," she said breathlessly.

Pol stood with his hands on his hips, his cock already pressing out the seam of his jeans. "Why don't we blindfold her and make her take the first one of us she finds?"

Cas' already hard cock lifted another inch. "I think that is a good idea."

"She'll strip first, of course."

Cas could see the pulse pounding in Fiona's throat, beckoning his tongue. "What about Selena? She might still be lurking."

Pol shook his head. "We could sense her if she was. And smell her foul scent. She was here, but she has gone. Something frightened her off, but I don't know what."

"The cat."

Cas frowned. Fiona looked at a point in mid-air, like she saw something he couldn't. "Cat?"

"The cat drove her away, like in the library."

Cas exchanged a glance with his brother. Fiona must be more tired than they thought.

"What cat?" Pol asked.

She looked surprised. "In the pottery room. The gray one."

He and Pol looked at each other again. "We saw no cat."

Fiona gaped at them then her look became thoughtful. "Oh."

"It was a long drive," Pol said, his smile returning. "She should take off her clothes now and put on the blindfold."

"Lock the door," Fiona said hastily. "I'd just die if anyone came in."

* * * * *

Cas thought he'd seen nothing sexier in the world than Fiona, completely bare, her toes splayed on the board floor, her arms outstretched while she tried to find the elusive twins. A white cloth bound her eyes and lifted her red hair, and she smiled as she groped her way around the room.

Her breasts were round and taut and moisture glistened on the twist of red hair at her quim. Her hips were shapely, and he remembered the smoothness of her skin there. Damn, this would take too long.

The twins had decided that not only did she have to find one of them, she had to identify him without removing the blindfold. Cas had pulled off his clothes, skin tingling in anticipation of being touched by her sweet, questing hands.

Now she reached toward him as though feeling his warmth and he sidestepped, suppressing his laughter so she wouldn't hear him.

Pol circled her from behind. Every so often, he'd dart in close, slap her on her backside and retreat before she could swing around and touch him.

"Oh, come on, that's not fair," she said when he did it again. "At least make some noise so I have *some* chance."

Pol let out a snicker. Fiona lunged at him, coming up with her hands against his torso. He stood there silently grinning while Fiona roved her fingers all over his body. Cas saw her brows furrow under the blindfold while she tried to decide which twin she'd caught.

His cock lifted high as she skimmed her hands down Pol's waist and hips and moved over his erection. She deliberately tested out its size and shape while Pol closed his eyes and suppressed a groan.

Cas slid his fingers over his own cock, pressing it in sympathy. He needed that bottle of oil Pol had obtained in Litohoro, the kind that smelled like lavender and complimented Fiona's own scent.

He bit back a raw sound as Fiona sank to her knees, her hands on Pol's hips, and drew Pol's cock into her mouth.

Cas watched her red lips stretch over it, watched Pol snake his hand through her hair, still holding himself back.

Fiona withdrew and licked Pol's cock all over, pausing now and then as though assessing his taste.

"Pol," she announced.

"You have it." Pol lifted the blindfold and guided his cock back in her mouth. Cas stroked his own in the same rhythm.

"How did you know?" Cas asked, walking toward them, hand still on his cock.

Fiona sent him a triumphant smile. "You taste different."

"Do we?"

She nodded. "You're smooth, like wine," she told Cas. "Pol is more like—schnapps."

Cas blinked. "What is schnapps?"

"Liquor with a bite, best drunk chilled."

Pol pretended to look horrified. "I hope you don't plan to chill me."

"No." She slanted him a wicked smile. "I like you warm."

Their shy Fiona was learning how sexy she was.

Cas moved to Pol's side. "Drink both of us," he suggested.

Fiona gazed up at him, lips parted, as though he'd just offered her the chalice of ambrosia from Zeus' table. "Can I?"

"I don't know, can you?" Pol grinned.

He moved closer to Cas, resting his arm on Cas' shoulder. *Double trouble*, that's what the gods of the Pantheon called them. Humans spun stories of Cas' and Pol's loyalty to each other, but the gods knew the truth.

Hell on wheels, Fiona had called them when she'd scolded them for riding Hans' bike too fast. Cas should explain to her that they had nothing to do with hell or even Hades. They were demigods of the heavens, of the paradise of Olympus.

Fiona was smiling as though she'd found paradise. She closed her mouth over Pol's cock, a look of rapture on her face. Then she backed away from him, turned her head, and took Cas'.

Cas' head rocked back. Oh yes, this *was* heaven. His fingers tightened on Pol's arm, and Pol held him upright, laughing softly.

"She's good, isn't she?"

"She is perfection," Cas corrected him.

Fiona went back and forth—Pol and Cas, Cas and Pol. Her mouth was hot and wet and made Cas crazy. Every time she drew away, he wanted to grab her and drag her back, and he knew Pol wanted the same. He wanted to haul her to the bed and fuck her, him alone, to tell her who she belonged to first.

At the same time, he wanted Pol to enjoy himself as well. His brother did, grunting as she slid her mouth over him, moving his hips to fuck her mouth.

Cas felt the buildup behind his balls that meant he was going to come. Fiona turned her mouth to him but he stepped out of the way.

Pol looked at him like he'd gone crazy. Cas shook his head. "Not yet. I want to do something else. Pol, let her drink from you on the bed."

Pol grinned slowly, knowing what Cas had in mind, and moved away from Fiona's questing mouth. She looked disappointed but then interested as Pol seated himself on the narrow bed and spread his legs, his feet dangling on either side of it.

Fiona brightened. She enjoyed gazing at Pol spread out like a feast, if the look on her face was anything to go by. When Pol beckoned to her with both hands, she went readily, smiling.

"On your hands and knees," Cas said. "Take him with your mouth."

Fiona obeyed. She crawled onto the bed and lowered her lips to cover Pol's cock, her ass raised.

That's what he wanted. Cas found the bottle of oil, smoothed it over his ready and hot cock, then climbed behind her.

He wouldn't take her ass, that was for Pol. Fiona's pussy, on the other hand, had been made for Cas.

Cas placed his hands on her hips, positioned himself at her opening and slid himself inside in one firm stroke.

Gods, yes. As before, their senses connected. He experienced her wonder and heart-pounding excitement to feel his cock in her, and he experienced his own excitement of her squeezing down on him.

At the same time, through her, he connected with what she was doing with Pol. He felt Pol's building urgency and the heat of her tongue as it brushed over Pol's flange. It was like fucking her and being sucked on at the same time.

He knew three would be better than one-on-one. He knew Pol felt what he did, the intense stimulation of her mouth on him and the feel of being inside her pussy.

And Fiona felt all of it. She began to writhe and squeal, trying to keep sucking on Pol while wanting to scream her ecstasy at what Cas was doing to her.

"That's it, baby," Pol said, swirling his hand through her fire-red hair. "Keep on it. Make me come."

She wriggled and moaned in her throat. Cas heard deeper moans and realized they came from him.

Gods, having her was better than anything ever had been in his entire existence. *Sweet Fiona, you were made for loving.*

She loved being fucked by them, plus she *worried* about them and tried to protect them. She was their champion, the woman who rescued them and faced down Selena for them.

Love you, baby. Love you.

He groaned and came. Pol came at the same time, and so did Fiona. The three of them spiraled to excitement together, Cas' blood pounding with it.

He felt her pussy squeeze him hard, felt her tongue all over Pol's cock, felt her ecstasy pumping through her body. He'd never had this connection before with any woman, and he knew that this meant she had been made for him.

And Pol.

Maybe Dionysus was looking out for them after all.

* * * * *

They slept after that, the three laid out on Fiona's bed, Cas holding her back against him while Pol snored on her other side. He breathed her fragrance as he slid into sleep, then he dreamed of making love to her.

They were on an island of golden sand while the blue, blue Mediterranean spread out before them, and he made love to Fiona on a beach. Pol lounged nearby, watching them while he sunned his naked body, his feet washed by the mild sea.

He seemed to hear the voice of his half sister, Artemis, daughter of Zeus and twin of Apollo. "Finally got it right, did you, Cas?"

The voice was so clear that he awoke. Nothing stirred in the room, save for the faint breeze at the window.

Cas softly kissed Fiona's cheek, and her eyelids fluttered. "Ah, you are awake," he whispered.

She smiled and turned her head for a kiss.

Cas made love to her then and there, entering from behind her, barely moving on the bed. It was slow, warm sex rather than the frantic frenzy they'd shared before.

On her other side, Pol awoke, smiled when he saw what they were doing, and joined in, playing with Fiona's breasts and quim until she was moaning and squirming between them.

Once Cas had climaxed, she took Pol in her mouth and finished him, all without them moving from the bed.

The full moon, Artemis' symbol, poured over the bed as they drifted to sleep again, and Cas swore he heard his half sister laugh.

* * * * *

When Fiona walked onto the site the next morning, everything seemed to be as normal. Archaeologists rose early because morning shadows were best for finding artifacts, and as usual, the dig was teeming at sunrise.

The smell of hot coffee beckoned her to an urn and she poured herself a cup. Hans was already hovering over his new *stoa* with Dr. Wheelan looking over his shoulder. Joan and Bob Whittington stood over a drawing spread across a bench, arguing with each other. All was normal.

When anyone glanced up and saw her in her work shorts and t-shirt, they either nodded good morning or waved, but other than that ignored her. Again, all as usual. Everyone was buried in their own tasks.

If they knew that Fiona had spent the night alternatively making love to two men and having Cas' cock in her while she sucked on Pol spread before her, they made no sign. Digs were such fonts of gossip—archaeology was a small world in many ways—that she was amazed no one seemed to know anything.

When the gray cat rubbed her ankles, she suddenly understood. Or thought she did. Had the cat stood guard outside the door and made sure none disturbed them all night?

Fiona still didn't know who the gray cat really was and if the creature was truly on their side. But she was keeping Selena away from them, and for that Fiona found the cat a strip of bacon and fed it to her.

Fiona had left Pol and Cas sleeping, one face up and one facedown, looking damn enticing with the sheet tangled around their brown legs, torsos bare to the morning sun. She'd studied them a moment before she left, Pol's black hair falling over his outstretched arm, Cas' lips curved as he smiled in his sleep.

Fiona tried to banish the smile from her own lips as she walked across the dig to Hans and Dr. Wheelan.

"Fiona." Dr. Wheelan gestured to her absently. "Another representative of the Greek antiquities department came about the jar. They want to see it. I offered them coffee." He peered at the site, which was empty of any official-looking Athenian. "I suppose they're about somewhere. Are you all right, my dear? You look pale."

"Just need my coffee," Fiona said breathlessly. She turned away, scooped up the gray cat and headed for the pottery room. The cat didn't seem to mind. It relaxed against Fiona's shoulder and purred.

Fiona reached the pottery room and tentatively pushed open the door. She wasn't certain what she was going to do if Selena was there—throw the cat at her?

She opened the door. A middle-aged man in a brown suit straightened up from studying a row of shards. "Hello," he said.

"Hello." Fiona clutched the cat, wondering if the man would suddenly morph into a black-leather clad Selena.

He didn't look as though he meant to. "I have been hearing about this vessel you have put together from the time of Pericles," he said in accented English. "I hear that it has a marvelously clear, intact painting. May I see it?"

He seemed genuine enough—in fact, she thought she recognized him from one of the many functions she'd gone to at the university when they'd first arrived.

Fiona held the cat a little more firmly and pointed toward the table. "Sure. It's over there."

Her hand froze, finger rigid. The gentleman looked in the direction she indicated and waited, puzzled. "Where?"

Words died on Fiona's lips. The table was empty, the jar gone. She glared accusingly at the cat, who looked back at her with unblinking orange eyes and kept on purring.

Chapter Twelve

ഉ

"This is a complete disaster! Why aren't you worried?"

Fiona stood with hands on hips and glared down at the twins who still lounged in her bed. They certainly looked like gods now, reclining half covered with her sheet, regarding her with lazy eyes.

"There is nothing to worry about, Fiona," Cas began.

"Yes, there is. Someone stole the jar! Selena most likely." She pointed an accusing finger at the cat, who'd followed her in. "*You* were supposed to guard it."

Pol pushed hair out of his eyes and looked around sleepily. "Who are you talking to?"

"The cat. Don't you see it? It's right there."

Fiona kept her finger trained on the cat who watched her without expression. Cas lifted his brows. "No. But if you say there is a cat, we believe you."

He and Pol exchanged a glance that maddened her.

"I know you think I'm crazy and that's just *fine*." She said it in a tone that let them know it was *not* fine. "There is a cat I can see and you can't, I'm having a ménage a trois with two demigods, and a magic jar has just been stolen by a demon demigoddess in dominatrix attire. Why should anyone think I'm crazy?"

"Fiona," Cas began.

"Don't start with me. The pair of you seducing me and making me play Blind Man's Bluff in the buff and then making me feel like *that*—and then you lay there calmly when all hell has broken loose. If she breaks that jar, you're dead. And I'll lose you."

She said the last with tears in her eyes. She loved them. Both of them. She loved them fiercely and if she lost them, the grief would hurt like nobody's business.

"Fiona," Cas said. "Hush, sweetheart. Selena didn't steal the jar."

Fiona transferred her glare to him. "How the hell do can you be so sure?"

Pol propped himself on his elbows and the sheet slid from his body, revealing his brown bare limbs and flat pelvis. "Because we stole it."

Fiona had dragged in a long breath to shout some more, and she choked. "*What?*"

Cas said, "Selena is tricky, but we are trickier. We put it in a place she'll never find it."

"No one will ever find it," Pol added.

They looked so smug and so hot lying there with the sheet exposing their bodies, dark eyes gleaming, smiles sinful.

Fiona moaned, sank to the foot of the bed and buried her face in her hands.

"Love?" Cas sat up put his arm around her. "We thought you'd be happy. You don't have to worry about it now. We'll take care of it *and* Selena."

Pol remained on his back and brushed the base of her spine with his toes. "You go back to digging up the Agora and finding your bits of pots. We can even tell you what they are."

Cas rubbed her shoulders as though trying to soothe her. He pressed a kiss to the top of her head.

"You can't steal an artifact," Fiona moaned. "It's illegal. People are very touchy about artifacts disappearing from the country in which it was found—and with good reason."

"But there are so many pots," Pol argued. "We'll find you another one."

"That isn't the *point.* Greece and England have been arguing about the return of the Elgin Marbles for *two hundred years.* If even a fragment of an artifact goes missing, it's a crime. I'll be arrested."

Cas actually chuckled. "You will not, Fiona, we will see to it."

"This isn't funny. I know you don't understand a lot of things because this isn't your century, but I know you saw prisons for people who broke the law. They'll keep me in jail here as an example of what happens to artifact stealers, and I'll never see the light of day again. Even if they do let me go, it will destroy my career."

"Baby." Pol sat up behind her and smoothed his fingers through her hair. "They won't arrest you."

"It was such a good career. Doing what I loved with people I like and respect…"

"We do have *some* powers, Fiona," Cas said. He cradled her against his chest. "We're demigods. We can make it so that no one but us notices the jar is gone at all. They will see what they want to see, hear what they want to hear."

Fiona looked up at him. His handsome face was dark with unshaved whiskers, his brown eyes liquid. She suddenly wanted to do nothing more than sit on this bed and kiss him, damn the jar, damn her career.

"We can't hide it forever," she said weakly.

"But long enough to deal with Selena," Pol rumbled. "Then you can have your pot back."

"How do you plan to deal with Selena?"

"Find her and kill her," Pol answered. "She is powerful, but so are we."

Fiona bit her lip. "I have the feeling it won't be that easy."

"You leave it to us."

Her anger rose. "Don't worry my pretty little head about it, you mean? I have to worry—you two are involved." She made an exasperated noise. "Besides, she put a binding spell on you. If you kill her, will that release the spell? Or just enforce it? I have the feeling she's put a lot of booby traps on it."

Cas' brows skimmed upward. "*Booby* traps?"

"Tricks and things so that if you try to release it or hurt her or whatever, the spell backfires and traps you even farther. Like if the pot breaks, you die or return to oblivion."

Pol traced her cheek. "You're sweet to be worried for us."

"I'm *not* sweet. I love you."

They stared at her.

"Which one of us did you say that to?" Cas asked, his voice quiet.

"Both of you." Fiona put her hands to her face. "I don't know why I said that. I have no idea what's wrong with me."

Cas rose from the bed, discarding the sheet. He was always so casual in his nakedness, as though clothes didn't matter. She supposed they didn't, not to a demigod.

"You love both of us?" He rested his hands on her shoulders and looked down at her. "In the same way?"

"I love you for different reasons. You, Cas, because you're feel things deeply and you soothe me and are so damn strong. Pol, because you are wild and wicked and make me do things I'd never dream of. But both of you just as intimately." She broke off. "I never thought I'd be saying this."

"Hey." Pol stepped behind her, also minus his sheet, his hands on her hips. "We're double trouble, sweetheart, opposite but equal. The twins of Gemini watch over those who are torn between opposites, the creative and the practical. We are completely different from one another, yet exactly the same."

"I know," Fiona said. "It drives me crazy."

"So take both of us," Cas breathed as he kissed her. "We like to share."

He licked the side of her neck, and at the same time, Pol leaned down and drew his tongue up the other side.

"You are trying to distract me."

"Is it working?" Pol asked.

It was. She felt her juices pool in her pussy and longed to throw one of them on the bed and impale herself on him.

That was the only thing that would satisfy her right now, one of their cocks deep inside her.

Perform the ritual.

Fiona jumped. The voice had been female and had sounded loud and clear in the room. Cas and Pol seemed not to have heard. They continued to kiss her neck, one on either side, satin hair brushing her, Pol reaching around and cupping her breast.

No one was in the room but them. And...

Fiona looked down and saw the cat at her feet. It sat on its haunches and stared up at her with unblinking eyes.

"What?"

Cas drew away, frowning slightly. Pol paid no attention.

Perform the ritual, the woman's voice came again.

Why don't you talk out loud? Fiona demanded mentally. *They think I'm nuts.*

I am a cat. I can only meow in my present form and make various kinds of rumbling noises. Would you prefer me yowling and you pretending you understood?

Who are you? Fiona asked, frustrated.

No one important right now. You are the important woman in this room, Fiona McCarty. You can save them if you perform the ritual.

What ritual? Fiona began, but suddenly she knew. "The ritual on the jar?" she asked out loud.

Precisely.

"Why will that save them?"

Cats could not smile, but Fiona swore this one did. *Trust me,* she said and then vanished.

"Fiona." Pol was regarding her with a patient expression. "Who are you talking to this time?"

"No one at all," Fiona said. She took Pol's hand and placed it where it had been on her breast, then took Cas' in hers, and while he slanted her a wicked smile, placed it between her legs.

* * * * *

Cas thought paradise could not be better than this. Fiona stood naked in front of them while he and Pol rubbed her down with oil. Pol's cock stood out achingly hard and Cas felt the same ache from his own.

She seemed adamant to perform the ritual he and Pol had done with Selena all those thousands of years ago. The difference between then and now was that neither Cas nor Pol had wanted to touch Selena, but they leapt at the chance to share this intimacy with Fiona.

Her shyness remained, but she had also learned her power. She stood still, her feet a little apart, a dreamy smile on her face as Pol oiled her thighs and Cas rubbed fragrant oil all over her breasts, pausing to pinch her nipples into pointed, tight nubs.

When they were all together, three as one, she would feel them feeling her, and Cas would feel what she and Pol felt. The joining would be nothing like he'd ever experienced, because this was Fiona, a woman he deeply loved.

Because he loved her, he had no trouble sharing her with Pol. Pol made her feel good in a different way from Cas, and Cas would never deprive Fiona of the pleasure his brother could give her.

No other man would touch her, but Pol was his twin, like an extension of himself. He grinned as he thought this, knowing that Pol would loudly refute the description.

They tied Fiona's wrists in front of her with a scarf. Pol lifted her, his arms around her waist, and Cas hooked his hands under her knees and parted her thighs. Standing against the cool wall, he eased Fiona onto him.

She moaned softly as he penetrated her. She leaned back and Pol held her, allowing Cas to enter her deeply.

She was hot and tight and welcoming. He felt love and excitement pouring from her, felt her walls closing on him, and sensed her own feelings of being penetrated. She writhed, loving it, and she loved it even better when Pol slid his hand around her and stroked her clit.

"You like that, sweetheart?" Pol asked.

She gave an incoherent reply. Cas pumped gently, needing to ease her open, while Pol began to massage and soothe her for what was to come.

The original ritual had been fast and harsh. Selena had laughed and gloated in her power, while Cas had felt nothing but disgust. What she'd done had been no less than rape.

With Fiona the excitement was nearly unbearable. Cas needed to go slowly, to ready her and not come until it was time. But she was so damn tight and felt so good that he began to pulse quickly, ready to spill his seed.

He forced himself to take deep breaths, to hold himself back. Pol still needed to loosen her, though she was already relaxing, her body wanting it.

She was so beautiful when caught in sexual pleasure. Her breasts were swollen, areolas dark and tight. Her skin thrummed with warmth, her pulse speeding, her eyes half-closed. Her red hair spilled over her shoulders and fanned over Pol's brown skin.

"Fiona," Pol breathed, his body tight and ready.

"It's good, she feels so good."

Pol smiled, knowing full well what Cas was experiencing. "Are you ready, Fiona?"

Fiona hesitated, looking back at him, her face flushed. "I don't know."

"You're nice and wide for me," Pol reassured her. "Do you remember how we did it at the inn?"

"Yes."

"This will be much the same."

Cas hugged her to him, still buried inside her. Pol moved behind her, stroking her back, soothing her. Her legs were already around Cas' hips, holding him tight.

Pol parted her buttocks with his hands, rubbing and massaging, opening her wider. Cas felt what Fiona felt, the hard firmness of Pol's tip slowly working its way inside.

He felt the burning fire, the slight pain, then the relaxation and the wonderful sensation of being filled. Pol pressed in, and in, and in. Fiona's mind clouded with the double feeling of Cas in her quim, Pol in her ass. They stretched and widened her, but she remained still, not fighting it.

"That's it, love," Cas murmured. "You're taking both of us."

"You're doing it beautifully," Pol added.

Fiona could not answer. Cas felt her mind swirl with dark pleasure, the feelings unimaginable. He felt Pol's growing excitement as she squeezed him hard, like a mirror of what she was doing to Cas' cock.

"Fuck," Pol groaned.

"Yes," Cas responded.

The twins felt her as one. Cas felt both her quim and her ass around his cock and Pol's. Her oiled breasts rubbed his chest and he felt her leaning back against Pol. He tasted her lips on his, and he tasted her hair as Pol licked and nibbled her neck.

He could no longer tell where his sensations left off and Pol's began. They were one now, no longer separate.

Cas also experienced Fiona's pleasure. The two were buried deep, rubbing each other through the walls of her. Her pussy pulsed around his cock, and she screamed her pleasure.

She raised her bound hands overhead, just like in the painting of them and Selena, opening herself to being fucked fully and deeply by both of them.

The walls of the plain room whirled around and dissolved into nothing. Darkness took its place, with thousands of stars overhead. Cas had no idea where they were. Mount Olympus? In the heavens?

Pol's eyes were tightly closed, his hands firmly gripping Fiona's hips. They floated in mid-air, the three of them joined forever. This is what Selena had wanted, the endless, mindless joy of the twins sealed together, feeling everything as one. But it hadn't worked.

Fiona writhed and pulsed between them, her orgasms beginning. "You're both so deep," she moaned. "Gods, you'll tear me apart."

"No," Cas said, kissing her face. "Never."

"You're tearing *me* apart, sweetheart," Pol said, his face shining with sweat. "She's so sweet. I'm going to come."

"With me," Cas urged. "With me."

"Hurry."

"Almost." Cas was going crazy. Fiona's orgasms blotted out her thoughts, leaving nothing but sensation. He'd never felt pleasure like this in his existence, and he'd existed a very long time.

Pol opened his eyes. Cas saw him notice the darkness and the stars stretching to eternity. "What the fuck?"

"Now," Cas said. He gripped Pol's shoulders and counted down. "Three, two, one."

His orgasm slammed into him like a powerful fist. He threw back his head as hot darkness took him and squeezed him hard. No, that was Fiona, taking his come. She screamed, and he felt the hot seed streaming into her both from himself and Pol.

He couldn't take it, it was killing him — it was the best thing that ever happened to him.

Cas pumped until he could pump no more. He gathered her close, his arms half around her, half around Pol's hard body. Pol moaned and pressed straight up inside her, his eyes shut tight.

Fiona's screaming wound down to wordless sounds, and she collapsed against his chest, her warm hair streaming over him.

The black of space and bright stars spun again and suddenly they were back in Fiona's bedroom, standing on the cool board floor where they had started.

Pol gently backed out of Fiona, his cock still partly stiff, and held her. From the jumble of hands and arms and bodies, he raised his head and looked at Cas, brown eyes full. "Thank you," he said.

Cas didn't answer and knew he didn't need to.

Fiona opened her eyes and looked up sleepily. "That was..." She let out her breath in a happy sigh. "Now what happens?"

Cas smoothed her hair. "Now we rest."

"Mmm, that sounds nice."

Pol laughed. "And then we do it again."

* * * * *

Three more times that day, Cas and Pol made love to Fiona. She was surprised she could stand so much, but she wasn't arguing.

The second time, Cas held her and penetrated her while Pol did nothing but touch her, then Pol took her while Cas held her and stroked her.

They did a threesome again, this time on the bed, Cas on one side, Pol on the other. In that position, they fell asleep and woke again when it was dark. They shared some food and a bottle of wine Cas had saved, departed to the separate bathrooms to shower, then returned, refreshed, and performed the ritual standing again.

The feeling of the three of them together amazed Fiona. She'd always wondered what men felt when they made love to a woman. She'd been unprepared for the sharp stab of excitement, the surging buildup to one incredible climax.

She'd screamed when they had, felt what they felt, over and around her own exquisite climax.

When they fell asleep after the third time, she'd barely had enough energy to kiss them good night. She'd have to take the day off and sleep to recover.

In the morning, however, the resilient twins had gone, and Fiona dragged herself, bleary eyed, to the showers. She should really put some time in at the dig, regardless of her need to help the twins and avoid Selena.

Why the cat had thought the ritual would help, she had no idea, but she admitted the wonderful love and sex that had surrounded her all night had been worth it.

Only one woman was in the showers this morning, behind a dangling curtain, probably Joan.

"Good morning," Fiona murmured, then brushed her teeth, stripped off her nightshirt, and stepped under the welcoming hot water.

The woman in the next shower zipped back her curtain and came charging into Fiona's stall.

It was Selena. She was naked and wet from the shower, her black hair sleek against her head. Her long, clawed fingers closed around Fiona's neck and pinned her to the wall.

"You should have stayed in bed," Selena hissed, and then the shower room disappeared.

Chapter Thirteen

ॐ

Fiona quickly learned the difference between having her wrists tied by a soft scarf for a round of pleasurable sex and having them tied in cruelty.

Leather bonds bit into her skin, her arms twisted behind her in at a painful angle. She lay on her side on a cold stone slab, exposed to a leaden sky. She had no idea where she was, but it looked like a ruined site of some ancient Greek temple.

Most sites today had tourists poring over them or archaeologists and historians picking over them bit by bit. Few lay deserted and empty, but this one did.

Selena leaned over her, whip in hand, black hair falling like a shimmering curtain. She dragged her fingers over Fiona's smooth hip. "I understand why they like you, Fiona. You're beautiful."

Selena had run her hands all over Fiona's naked body, dipping into intimate places while Fiona struggled against her bonds. Selena's palm moved now on her hip and Fiona bit back nausea.

"Stop touching me," she growled.

Selena smirked. "Only like demi*gods*, do you?" She gave Fiona's backside a tiny slap with the whip. "We need to do *something* to keep us busy until they get here."

Anger welled up inside Fiona, hot and intense. "I *said*, stop touching me."

A fiery spark jumped from Fiona's body to Selena, knocking the demigoddess a few feet back. Selena scrambled to her feet, blinking, surprised.

Then a slow smile curved on her face. "They gave you some of their powers, did they? How sweet."

Fiona tried to catch her breath. "What are you talking about?"

The surge of power had been unexpected and frightening, but at the same time she tasted triumph. She was not the helpless ninny Selena thought her.

"When they shared you. When the three of you became one, you absorbed some of their power."

Fiona lay still, not wanting the demigoddess to know the extent of her bewilderment. Was that why the cat, whoever she was, told Fiona to perform the ritual? So she would acquire some of the twins' power?

That didn't feel right. The twins were magical, but subtly so. They simply wanted people to do things for them and people did. Their power was the extension of their charm.

This power felt raw and sparkling. Was it the twins who had given it to her or the ritual itself?

"It will be fun to test how strong you are," Selena said, folding her arms over her ample bosom. "It will pass the time until they get here."

"How do you know Cas and Pol will do what you want?"

Selena smirked. "Oh please. I sent them a message they'll understand. They bring me the jar or I kill you. Simple."

"They will never give you back the means to hold them prisoner."

"Yes, they will. I've been watching them, Fiona. They like you. In fact they've gotten all sappy and sentimental over you. They'll bring the jar." Selena sat down cross-legged next to Fiona and raised her whip. "In the meantime, let's see what makes Fiona spark."

* * * * *

"If we give her the jar, it's back to oblivion for us," Pol said.

Cas held the terracotta pot in his hands, rescued from where they'd hidden it in Hans' *stoa* in the Agora. They'd concealed it among other pottery reserved for Fiona and made the others simply not notice it.

He studied the black painted picture of himself and Pol, their arms folded, facing away from each other. He said quietly, "If we don't take it to her, Fiona will die."

"I know."

The two men stared at one another. Cas saw in Pol's eyes that they'd already made their choice. They could not let anything happen to Fiona.

"I will miss her," Cas said.

"You think I won't?"

Cas wrapped the jar carefully in the sheets Fiona had used to cushion it. He placed it in the carryall on Hans' motorcycle then lifted his helmet over his head. "I do not suggest we go tamely back to Selena. We fight her."

"I'm not doing twenty-five hundred years in the dark with you again."

Cas grinned tightly. Pol would fight to the death.

They mounted the bike, Cas cranked it to life and they shot out into Athenian traffic.

Somehow he knew exactly where to go. He headed through the crowded streets, Pol clutching him and starting to curse again, and bore north, toward Delphi.

He and Pol had left the Agora that morning and returned to wake up Fiona. They'd enjoyed themselves discussing ways they could rouse her from sleep as they walked, each idea more cock-hardening than the last.

When they reached her corridor of the dorm, they'd found a gray cat with orange eyes pacing in an agitated manner outside the bathroom.

She's taken her, a woman's voice had projected into their minds. *She got past me, and I discovered her too late. I'm sorry.*

Cas stared at the cat, feeling its terrible anger and distress.

"Who the hell are you?" Pol asked.

I can't reveal myself until it's all over. I promised, damn Dionysus anyway. But if she kills Fiona, it will be all over for you, my friends. And I won't be able to stop it.

Cas' own anger built into a murderous rage. Selena would not last the day. If she harmed Fiona he would risk Poseidon's wrath and kill her. Slowly.

They'd left the cat behind and gone down to the Agora to fetch the jar. Now Cas sped into the countryside of Greece, overtaking busses and cars speeding along toward the tourist Mecca of Delphi.

Selena would not have gone to Delphi itself, Cas reasoned, because she would not risk facing Apollo. The entire area was dedicated to the worship of Apollo, and Cas knew that twenty-five hundred years would not have diminished the god's fierce possessiveness. Any mortal or half-mortal who challenged Apollo had always come to a nasty end, and Cas doubted the god had changed.

He instinctively knew to turn west before they reached Delphi. Selena had taken Fiona deep into the mountains where most travelers did not go. He left the main roads and drove the motorcycle across dirt tracks and through rutted gullies, the air growing ever cooler as they climbed.

Pol nudged him from behind and pointed a long arm toward a bowl-like depression just north of them. Cas couldn't hear him over the roar of the bike but he understood.

They left the narrow track he'd been using and shot off across the fields, scaring a handful of goats and earning the glare of an elderly goatherd. Pol clung harder as the motorcycle slipped and slid down the incline and through a stand of trees.

The bike slid out from under him when it hit a hidden slab of stone. Cas had been going fairly slow over the slippery terrain, so he and Pol didn't fall very hard. They rolled away from the bike, greenery tearing as they slid to reveal an ancient marble floor.

The motorcycle sputtered and died. Cas yanked off his helmet but heard nothing but the empty silence of the ruin. A few stones stood on the periphery of the marble floor and that was all.

"A temple." Pol wiped gravel from his hair and tossed his helmet aside. "Recognize it?"

"No." Cas scanned the area, but this Greece was different from the one he'd roamed thousands of years ago, bent on mischief and fun. Now the beautiful marble and stone buildings lay ruined and abandoned, and metal and the new substance called *plastic* ruled the day.

He made his way back to the motorcycle and lifted the jar out of the metal saddle bag. The jar was unhurt, as he assumed, since he and Pol were still intact.

"She's here," Pol stated. "I can feel it."

"Yes."

Cas cocked his head, trying to listen, trying to sense Fiona's whereabouts. He was connected with her as he'd been connected with no other woman, human or goddess, in his long life.

But he heard nothing. The silence of the place, forgotten and neglected, bore down on him. The call of birds sounded faintly among the trees, drowned out by the wind moaning across the ruin.

Then, faintly behind the wind, came a sharp scream.

As one Pol and Cas sprinted across the slippery ivy-covered marble toward the corner of the ruin. They heard a second scream, followed by a high-pitched laugh. Then the laugh ended in a yelp.

"Oh, that was a good one," Selena's amused voice said.

At the end of the slab of marble was a square hole and a staircase leading down. The staircase was deep and narrow and worn smooth by time. Pol descended first, Cas coming behind, carefully carrying the jar.

The staircase opened into a high-ceilinged stone room, now buried, but once it must have been aboveground. Marble pillars marched along each wall, just holding back crumbling rock and dirt.

A gray light filled the room and showed carvings on the marble ceiling, scenes of sexual excess, grotesque renditions of what should be pleasurable. Bondage here meant cruelty, not the joy of surrender.

Fiona floated high on one pillar, her hands pinned behind her, her naked body surrounded by a greenish glow. Selena stood beneath her, her hands splayed, holding Fiona about twenty feet above the floor with her power.

Selena spoke to the twins without turning. "Aren't you going to say *let her go*?"

"We have the jar," Cas answered.

Selena laughed. She moved her hand and Fiona shot higher, her red head stopping just shy of the ceiling.

As Cas balled his fists a bright gold spark jumped from Fiona's body and arced down to strike Selena.

Selena screamed, and Fiona began to drop. Pol sprinted forward, but before Fiona hit the floor the nimbus caught her, and she floated upward again.

Pol got his hands around Selena's neck. Selena recovered from the jolt and lashed out with power, sending Pol hurtling backward across the room.

Cas set the jar carefully in a corner and helped Pol to his feet. "If we go at her together, we can do this."

Pol's dark eyes blazed fury. He wiped his mouth with the back of his hand and gave his brother a nod.

Selena put her hands on her hips. "Give me the jar, or she dies."

"Don't do it," Fiona shouted.

Cas heard rage in her voice rather than fear. Brave lady.

"Your choices really are all bad," Selena said. "If you succeed in killing me you'll be bound to the jar forever. Who knows what that means? Will you become mortal and die? Or will you go back into the painting, trapped forever on a piece of clay? And if you destroy the jar…" She made a slitting motion across her throat. "Back to oblivion for you."

"Oh, just kill her." Fiona glared down at the demon demigoddess. "She's too full of herself."

Pol laughed out loud. Together he and Cas rushed her, closing in on either side of her. Selena screamed as they bore her backward, and fought them like a cat.

Cas sensed the surges of power in Fiona but knew she didn't know how to control them. Another spark arced out from her body, but it caught Pol on its way to Selena.

Pol rolled away, and Selena cried out, but she did not receive enough of a jolt to slow her down.

"Stupid bitch," Selena snarled. "Can't even aim."

The demon demigoddess broke away from them and used her power to slam Fiona against the ceiling. Fiona's body pressed hard against the marble, right next to the portrayal of a satyr ravishing a screaming maiden.

"I'll kill her." Selena's voice was hard but calm. "I've been toying with her up until now, but I'll kill her and summon demons to eat her flesh if you don't bring that jar to me."

"Get it yourself," Pol growled.

"No." Selena's voice rang out, making Cas wonder why she was so adamant. Would the spell not work if she had to fetch the jar? What was she afraid of? "Give it to me and darling Fiona goes free."

Cas remained still. Her letting Fiona go "free" might mean dropping her from the ceiling, which was thirty feet above them. They would be trapped and Fiona would be dead or dying.

He could not let Selena win. Fiona's power was strong, crackling like lightning, but she did not know how to use it, however the hell she had acquired it.

He shared a glance with Pol. Together they ran at Selena again and bore her against the wall. She easily threw them off, slamming Fiona back against the ceiling with a wave of her hand, but a strange thing happened.

Selena—*chipped*. A small piece of her cheek fell from her and shattered on the floor, becoming dust. Selena slapped her hand to her face, and when it came away her cheek had reshaped itself.

Cas frowned, thoughts spinning in his head. Selena had disappeared from the jar. Fiona's newfound power hurt her. Part of her skin had chipped like a piece of old clay.

He ran at her again, grabbing her arm and slamming her against the wall. He grinned savagely as she shrieked, another piece of her skin crumbling and falling to the floor.

It repaired itself immediately, but he knew now what he had to do, no matter what the cost, to keep Fiona safe from her. If they did not destroy her she'd grow stronger and stronger until nothing they could do would affect her.

Cas shared another glance with Pol. Pol had seen everything, and they didn't need to exchange words or even thoughts to understand each other.

Cas walked to the shadowy corner and picked up the terracotta jar. In the painting he and Pol looked grim, which reflected how Cas felt now.

Pol met him in the center of the floor. They took up a stance, back to back, just as in the painting. The Gemini twins, Castor and Pollux, the equal and the opposite, forever together.

Above them, Fiona caught on what they meant to do. "No," she screamed. "Cas, no, please."

Pol looked up at her and gave her a sad smile. "Love you, sweetheart."

Cas also sent her a smile, wishing he could touch her face and kiss her lips one last time. "I love you, Fiona," he said softly.

"No!" Sparks flew from Fiona's body and suddenly her hands were free. She pointed her fingers at Selena, but the power still eluded her, shooting past Selena and leaving a scorch mark on a random column.

Cas lifted the jar over his head and flung it hard against the floor. It connected with the marble and shattered into a thousand mute terracotta fragments. "Love you," he whispered.

He heard Fiona scream before darkness blotted out his world.

* * * * *

"No," Fiona sobbed as the twins vanished.

Selena turned her face upward. "You stupid bitch, you *told* them."

Tears streamed down Fiona's face, smearing the dirt already there. She had no idea what Selena was talking about, she only knew that the twins were gone and there was an unbearable void in her heart.

She reached out, trying to bring the power within her to bear, trying to focus it on Selena to destroy her. Sparks fizzled at her fingertips, guttering like a light bulb attempting to stay on. Selena laughed at her.

"It didn't work, and you can do nothing."

Fiona knew the truth of her words, though she was not certain *what* didn't work. She wished Cas could have told her what he meant to happen instead of simply vanishing. She had seen pieces of Selena crumble, but she did not know how to use that to her advantage. Where was the gray cat when Fiona needed her?

As soon as the image of the cat and its orange eyes formed in Fiona's mind Selena's laughter cut off abruptly.

The demon demigoddess let out a long keening wail, the cry of a being in unbearable pain, and her hands went to her face. Fiona watched in amazement as Selena's entire body split into tiny cracks, just like the jar. Crazed lines flowed all over her until she resembled a painted statue, poorly put together.

Fiona suddenly understood, or thought she did. Cas and Pol had risked that breaking the jar would shatter Selena, that so much of her magic had been put into the vessel that she could not survive without the jar. They had sacrificed themselves in order to destroy her.

Anger and power surged within Fiona, certain and strong, and she pointed it at the woman below.

"*Break*," she said quietly.

This time, she had no trouble directing the power. Sparks arced from her spread fingers and encased Selena.

The demigoddess exploded. Shards of pottery flew like bullets throughout the room, smashing into the walls and becoming nothing but dust. A few smacked Fiona's flesh but bounced harmlessly off her to grind to powder on the floor.

Fiona shielded her face as the shards danced around her, becoming smaller and smaller until they fell to the floor in a rain of fine dust.

Selena's magic vanished and Fiona plummeted downward. She screamed and screamed, pressing her hands out in front of her, desperately willing her body to stop.

She did stop about three feet from the floor. She hovered in midair as though a cushion had caught her, and she lay there, gasping.

When she caught her breath she swiveled her legs to press her feet to the floor, her heart still pounding.

The dank air was cold on her bare skin, but she scarcely noticed it. The shards that had been Selena had disintegrated to nothing, but the painted jar had broken into potsherds that remained scattered throughout the room. Hans' clothing, not magical, lay in two heaps, with two pairs of worn sandals next to them.

Fiona fell to her knees and gathered the pottery pieces to her, tears raining down her face.

She found a fragment of Cas' face on one, and she kissed and pressed it to her cheek.

They were truly gone.

She covered her face with her hands and gave herself over to grief. She'd loved them, Cas and Pol both. They'd granted her the gift of life, something she'd denied herself through her long years of study.

They'd made her come out of her shell and live. They'd made her be daring and bold and risk her heart. They'd taught her about wild and wicked sex, but they'd also made her see so much more. They'd looked on a world that was as strange to them as landing on Mars would be to her, and they'd embraced every aspect of it.

She sobbed into her hands, wetting the pottery fragment with her tears. "I love you," she whispered. "I love you."

Something brushed her foot and she jumped. But it was only the gray cat, staring up at her with orange eyes. It was breathing hard.

Fiona's anger surged. "I definitely do *not* want to see you right now. You could have stopped this."

Not really. You had to do it.

"They're dead and gone, consigned to oblivion. You told me to perform the ritual so it would give me power. You made them understand that to save me they had to destroy themselves."

I did all that? Goodness, I was prepared.

"I don't understand about Selena, though. Why did she crumble to dust? I thought that she was free of the jar."

No, she was stupid. She put so much of her power into the jar when she created it, that she essentially became the vessel. Her picture didn't disappear because she was out of it. It disappeared because her essence became it. The cat nudged a painted shard. *Without the jar, she couldn't hold herself together anymore.*

Fiona lifted the shard under the cat's paw. It was a fragment of Pol's painted shoulder, which made her tears flow again.

"Why did the twins have to die too? Why couldn't you save them? Why couldn't this power I gained save them?"

The power can save them. The power is the magical part of them that infused you during the ritual.

Fiona rubbed tears from her eyes. "How do I know how to use it? And don't tell me I have to search for the answer within myself, because I might have to throw you across the room."

The cat gave her a patient look. *Fiona, you are an archaeologist. A pottery specialist. Do you know what that means?*

She sniffled. "It means I'm underpaid, get my fingers dirty and have a permanent crick in my back."

How amusing. It means you know how to find obscure fragments of pottery and figure out how to put them together.

Fiona stared at the shards in her hands, then at the cat. "Oh goddess."

The cat intoned slowly, like she was teaching a child. *Put the jar together again, Fiona.*

"But…won't that revive Selena?"

What was on the jar when it broke?

"Pol and Cas."

What will be on it when you put it together?

"Pol and Cas. I hope."

The cat said nothing. It waited, tail curled around its feet, eyes still.

Fiona scrambled for fragments. "Help me find them. Hurry!"

The cat wasn't much help at all. She did bat a few of the pieces to Fiona then grimaced in cat daintiness and washed her feet.

Fiona put on one of the discarded shirts then almost cried again when she realized that Cas' scent lingered on it. Pushing tears firmly aside she pulled the fragments into a pile and then began figuring out where each would fit.

She worked well into the night. She had to leave once to find the motorcycle and a flashlight stashed in its saddlebag. She found a forgotten candy bar in there too, still wrapped, and ate it for the sugar rush.

Fiona knew her job. She had to be painstaking and patient, fitting each piece into its place, calmly setting aside what didn't fit until she could reason out what went where.

It was tedious work, and her hands were shaking with fear. What if she did it wrong or it didn't work or she couldn't find all the pieces?

That kind of thinking didn't solve problems, she told herself.

She lined up the pieces by shape and design, just as she did when putting together a simple amphora or perfume jar. She bent over her work, her back aching, her eyes straining to see in the gloom. She didn't dare carry everything out into the open, fearing she'd drop it or leave a vital piece behind.

The night grew cold. She covered herself with the clothes and kept on working. The cat curled up on her lap, warming itself and her at the same time.

Morning came, June sunlight penetrating the staircase opening and sliding across the marble floor. The cat woke, stretched and bounded off after a lizard. The slithering of the lizard made Fiona think of snakes and the fact that vipers existed in Greece. But she hadn't time to worry about things like that, either.

By midmorning, she had the jar assembled except for one piece. Her heart beat faster as she beheld the painting of Cas and Pol, standing back to back. There was a slight difference in the painting, and she had to lean close to detect it.

Whereas before the two had been scowling, now they wore looks of smug satisfaction.

"Hang on," she told them.

She steadied the jar as she groped around for the last missing piece, fearing the unstable jar would crumple in on itself. She had no glue handy, just dampness mixed with dust and the fact that the pieces fit together tighter than a jigsaw puzzle. The jar stayed together, to her surprise— perhaps the power that infused her from Cas and Pol was helping.

But she could not find the missing piece. She hunted all over for it, feeling her way across the slimy floor and pointing the flashlight into every corner. She had no way of knowing if it was just missing or had shattered to powder as the fragments of Selena had done.

Tears were flowing from her eyes again when the cat sat down in front of her.

Don't panic, it's right here.

The cat dropped a shard from its mouth. It wrinkled its nose then busily began to clean its face.

Fiona cared less that the shard was covered with dirt. She kissed it and set it into place and then sat back.

Nothing happened. Fiona clenched her hands, willing herself to be patient, but she waited and waited and waited. The strip of sunshine crawled across the floor. The cat yawned, tucked its feet under itself and closed its eyes.

Just when Fiona had decided the cat was wrong and putting the jar together did nothing, the vessel began to shake.

A faint glow surrounded it, then suddenly something reached into Fiona and yanked the electric power out of her body and into the jar. She screamed then clapped her hand over her mouth in case she upset the process by making noise.

The cracks sealed themselves, rendering the jar complete and whole, the painting glowing as brightly as it did when the potter had first painted it twenty-five hundred years ago.

A brilliant light burst from the jar, knocking Fiona flat on her back, and then — darkness.

Chapter Fourteen

ೞ

Fiona woke to whispers.

"She's so beautiful."

"And so sexy in a t-shirt and nothing else."

The first voice softened to a chuckle. "I saw her first."

"The fuck you did," Pol answered.

Fiona's eyes flew open. They lay nude on either side of her, stretched out in lazy contemplation. Cas had propped himself on his elbow and trailed his hand down the curve of her waist, while Pol lay on his back, one knee bent, running his foot sensually over her leg.

She gasped and sat up. "It worked."

"Told you it would."

Fiona stared across the room at a tall young woman with ringlets of blond hair held back by a bandeau. She wore a short blue tunic and sandals that laced up her slim legs and had a bow slung across her back. She lounged on a slab of stone, one foot dangling negligently, watching Fiona and the twins.

Fiona recognized her voice. "You were the cat."

"Yes, and I'm glad you *finally* figured everything out, because I was tired of all that fur. It needed constant attention."

Cas laughed softly. "I should have known a huntress would choose to be a cat."

"Who is she?" Fiona asked.

"Artemis," Pol answered for him. "Goddess of the hunt and the moon. What are you doing here?"

"Looking after my favorite half brothers. When Fiona began to unearth you a few years ago, I knew there was a chance to finally set you free."

Fiona sat up, anger surging. "You sat back while they were trapped and never helped them?"

She made a face. "I *did* help. I was thrilled when someone actually had enough interest to finish the jar, no matter how long it took. Once you brought them back, I kept Selena at bay and pointed you toward the right way to free them completely. Of course, I had to tell you point blank to perform the ritual. Humans can be so dense."

"That's what set them free of the jar, the magic I got from doing the ritual?"

"Almost." Artemis hopped to her feet, adjusting the bow. She was very tall for a woman, probably as tall as the twins, and moved with a leggy grace. "Selena was a half-demon, and demons are extremely self-centered. When she forced Cas and Pol to perform the ritual all those years ago, it was performed in anger on their part, gloating on hers. That's why the ritual backfired and trapped them in the painting on the jar. Not in ecstasy, but in oblivion."

"But when *we* performed it…" Fiona began.

"You performed it in love. The magic of their love filled you and helped you fight Selena. Then when you put the jar together, it returned to them to set them free. Selena's purpose was to trap them, but you wanted to free them, even if it meant you lost them. And you two." Artemis pointed a long finger at Cas and Pol. "You were ready to consign yourselves to oblivion to save Fiona's life."

"Worth it," Cas said.

"Well, good thing Fiona's a genius and or you'd still be pottery fragments."

Pol nuzzled Fiona's ear. "She has the magic of archaeology. Very powerful."

"It's science, not magic," Fiona protested.

Artemis scowled. "Humph, I always thought it was looting. That rude Heinrich Schliemann digging up the place and stealing everything not nailed down and thinking he found Agamemnon—he wasn't even close. The bronze age princes he did find were quite unhappy to have their burial goods stolen. Humans have such short memories— they believe if a culture has disappeared its spirituality is gone, too. It must be handicapping to see only one spectrum."

"She likes to lecture," Pol confided to Fiona.

"Why did you remain in cat shape?" Fiona asked her. "Selena would have been much more frightened if you had appeared in your true form."

Artemis rested one hip on the stone ledge behind her. The twins seemed unembarrassed to be naked in the goddess's presence, perfectly content to stroke Fiona's skin and press kisses to her in front of their sister.

"This isn't my true form, either," Artemis said. "I appear to you this way because you would not be able to handle looking at my true form. It might shock you to death, and Cas and Pol would be very upset with me. I was the cat because I couldn't interfere, not directly. There are rules."

Fiona raised her brows. "Remembering mythology, I'd say the gods interfered all the time."

"The stories are the exceptions about us fighting amongst ourselves. We guide, we advise, we protect. We don't do things *for* you. But now that you have figured things out, I can appear to you in a more understandable form and say goodbye."

Pol leisurely sat up. "You're leaving? Too bad. We found this taverna—you could dance the night away and slay the men who try to touch you."

She smirked. "*Nice*. Some of us have work to do."

Fiona climbed to her feet, hating to slide out from between the twins but wanting to be standing up, relatively clothed, in front of a goddess. "This might sound rude, but why did *you* come? Why the goddess of the moon? Why not Aphrodite, the goddess of love?"

Artemis barked a laugh that rang through the small temple. "Oh please. *She* wouldn't lift a finger if she thought it might ruin her manicure."

On the ceiling high above them, one of the overly lush, cavorting women suddenly turned her head and looked down. "I heard that."

"Not to mention she's always eavesdropping. Let's just say I wanted my brothers to be happy, and I had the feeling you'd make them happy." Artemis' face softened into a smile, which gave Fiona a glimpse of the incredible beauty she'd have in her true goddess form. "I like to see them happy. They're so cranky, otherwise."

"That's true," Pol agreed.

Artemis brushed off the back of her tunic. "You three go on now. I think I'll completely destroy this temple." She glanced at the vulgar paintings on the ceiling. "A temple to a demon demigoddess. What a waste. Humans need more to do."

Cas had already risen. Casually, he leaned over and pulled on his jeans, his thighs moving invitingly. "I'm happy to leave this place behind." He slanted a smile at Fiona. "I know this nice little inn near Mount Olympus."

Fiona blushed, remembering what had happened at the nice little inn near Mount Olympus.

Pol grinned. "I say we go."

Cas zipped and buttoned his jeans. He left off the t-shirt, because Fiona was wearing it. "I don't know if we can fit three on the bike."

"Or if it will even work after you dumped it in the ditch," Pol said.

"That was Selena's doing."

"Sure, blame a dead demon. You and I ride, Fiona. We'll make Cas walk."

Cas' dark eyes were warm as he smiled at Fiona. "We'll all get there. I promise."

Fiona dragged her gaze from the enticing Cas standing with hands on slim hips, wearing nothing but a pair of jeans, and noticed that Artemis had disappeared.

Pol hurriedly pulled on his clothes. "Time to go. If Artemis says she'll destroy this temple, she will, and it won't be pretty."

They went quickly up the stairs, Pol leading, Cas behind Fiona to help her up the slippery steps. Fiona had nothing to wear on her feet and she viewed the rock-strewn slopes in dismay, wishing Artemis could have conjured her some hiking boots.

Cas solved the problem by lifting her in his arms and carrying her across the slab of slippery marble and down to the ditch where they'd left the motorcycle.

Behind them, a small earthquake began. The three of them hunched behind an outcrop of rock while the temple collapsed on itself with a rumble, clouds of dust shooting skyward.

Fiona coughed as the dust came down. She peeped around the rock and saw nothing but a mound of crushed rock and dirt, ground too fine for an anyone to piece together again.

The archaeologist in her mourned the loss of the artifacts within the temple, but another part of her knew that some things were best left undisturbed.

The motorcycle was too small for three. Once Cas righted it and untangled ivy from it, Pol boosted Fiona onto it and handed her his helmet. "You two go," he said. "I'll meet you there."

Fiona snaked her arm around his neck and kissed him. "Thank you."

He slanted his mouth across hers, letting the kiss turn interesting, and finished by rubbing his palm across her breast. "I'll be there," he said. "Soon."

"Take your time," Cas answered.

Pol laughed as Cas started the bike. Fiona settled herself behind him and pulled on her helmet. She wrapped her arms around Cas' warm body, very happy to be going anywhere he took her.

And when Pol got there, he would be welcome too.

* * * * *

They spent two days at the inn with Mount Olympus rearing in the background. Fiona insisted she buy herself clothes, over Cas' and Pol's protests that she looked fine naked. She indulged herself in an embroidered cotton blouse and colorful skirt and a pair of new sandals. The outfit was very unlike her work clothes, and she felt pretty in them.

Besides, she could hardly go to cafés and tavernas in nothing but Hans' t-shirt. Cas and Pol insisted that they could stay in the bedroom constantly—no need to go out, but Fiona reminded them that humans got hungry.

The only slight worry in the orgy of delights that Cas and Pol gave her was what would happen next. Cas and Pol were immortal. She was not. The slight powers that the ritual had borrowed from Cas and Pol and put in Fiona were gone, and she reasoned that briefly sharing their power would not make her immortal as well.

She would have to return to her job and her life and they might not want to come with her, let alone watch her age and die.

Cas and Pol seemed untroubled by this dilemma. They lived for the day, never minding about tomorrow. They taught her so much in those two days, how to arouse them and herself and how draw out the pleasure until they drowned in it.

Fiona never dreamed she'd beg two men to tie her hands behind her back and let her bring them to readiness with her mouth alone. She never dreamed she'd let a man bend her over a windowsill and fuck her from behind. Thankfully the street had remained deserted, but the possibility that someone could walk around the corner and see her and Cas at any time had excited her quickly into climax.

After breakfast on the third day, Cas announced that he was going to journey up Mount Olympus again.

"Come with me, Fiona?"

Pol snorted and set down his coffee. "What do you want to go all the way up there for?"

"To find answers to a few questions." Cas drank his coffee, his throat moving with his swallow.

Pol lost his smile. "I was avoiding the questions."

"We cannot avoid them forever. Fiona?"

Fiona nodded, thinking she knew what Cas was going to do.

Later, she and Cas rode the motorcycle up the main roads to the mountain then left it behind in a parking lot and proceeded on foot. Pol met them at the trailhead. The secret of him getting around so fast wasn't much of a secret—he charmed his way into hitching rides with people.

They began the trek with other hikers, walking slowly. Fiona held both twins' hands, not wanting to let either go.

As before when she walked this mountain, she began to feel dizzy, then a fog descended over her and she closed her eyes.

When she opened them again, the three of them stood in the meadow high on the mountainside, and a stag was just coming to a stream to drink. They waited, still hand in hand, while the stag finished satisfying its thirst.

It raised its head and began to walk toward them, morphing as he did so into the man-shape in which Dionysus had presented himself to Fiona before.

"Immortals in love with a mortal woman," he said. "It's always a problem."

Cas slid his arm around Fiona's waist. It felt so natural to have him there beside her, warm and strong, a man who loved her.

Cas said, "If you're about to offer me a big choice—if you're about to say *Cas, would you give up your immortality for her?* my answer is *yes*. It's an easy question."

"Pretty easy for me as well," Pol said. "If Cas and Fiona are mortal, I will be too."

"Wait a minute," Fiona broke in. "You can't give up *immortality*. It's not the same thing as giving up—I don't know, the motorcycle."

"Oh, I'm keeping the motorcycle," Cas said. "I'm buying it from Hans."

Fiona faced him, exasperated. "Screw the motorcycle. Giving up immortality means growing old and *dying*. No more partying with the gods or floating around the constellations. It means working and hurting and having your strength fade. It means no more magic."

"It also means loneliness," Pol said.

Cas touched her face. "I would rather be mortal with you and do mundane things like work and eat and sleep than live forever without you. I want to be part of your life, not watch your life go by. And I wouldn't want to go on without you."

Fiona glanced at Pol, who nodded. "What Cas said."

"Fine," Dionysus interrupted.

Fiona raised her hands. "Wait. You can't take away their immortality. Not for me. The sacrifice is too much."

Dionysus gave her a patient look. "Is that what you truly wish?"

"Of course it is. I don't want them dying because of me."

"But we are *alive* because of you," Cas said. "You brought us back from the jar."

"I know I did. And I want you to go on being the demigods of good times. Always."

"What a sweetheart," Dionysus chuckled. "No more arguing. I've made my decision."

"What decision?" Fiona asked in suspicion.

"*My* decision. It would break my big god heart to see any of you pining for each other. The three of you will live out a mortal lifespan and when you die, you will *all* return to Mount Olympus to rejoin the Pantheon. All right?"

"We'll be mortal?" Pol asked.

"For a while. Starting right now."

Cas waited then frowned. "That is all? I do not feel any different."

"You will. But in about fifty years, you'll return to me and be demigods again. Castor and Pollux and their sexy demigoddess Fiona."

Pol cupped Fiona's backside. "Sexy demigoddess. I like it."

"I'll even fix it so you can both live as her life mates without the humans thinking there's anything odd," Dionysus said.

"Thank you," Fiona breathed. She twined her hand with Cas', her heart lightening. She would not have to lose them or make them choose between her and their own world.

"Hey, this is the fun part about being a god." Dionysus' eyes took on a wicked twinkle. "The other fun part is the orgies."

* * * * *

Back at the Agora a few days later, Hans Jorgensen pointed happily to a mostly intact jar he'd unearthed. "I thought you'd want to see this, Fiona."

The painting on the jar depicted a portion of a woman in a short tunic, her blonde hair wildly curling, running with her hunting bow. She seemed to be chasing an overly voluptuous female demon dressed all in black. The fragment of inscription that the potter had painted said, "Artemis pursues…"

Fiona chuckled. Hans glanced at her in surprise. "What is funny?"

"Nothing. Thank you, Hans. When it's ready, I'll move it to the pottery room."

She walked away from the *stoa* with a light heart. Somewhere Artemis was enjoying herself.

When she walked into her bedroom, she felt slightly uneasy, though she saw no one there.

Then the door slammed behind her. Before she could turn around, strong hands pinned her arms and a blindfold slid over her eyes.

"No," she protested. "I have to go back to work."

Hands unbuttoned her shorts and pushed them down. "Not without clothes, you don't," Pol whispered in her ear.

She started to laugh with dismay. She felt Pol's fingers at the waistband of her underwear, tugging it from her hips. "I think these should stay off."

"I agree," Cas said behind her. She felt his warmth, the length of his tall, unclothed body at her back, the rigid press of his cock.

"We played a blindfold game before," Pol breathed in her ear. "Remember? You had to tell us who you touched. This time, you get to tell us who is touching you."

"Oh." Fiona shivered in excitement, cream pooling in her quim, and the game began.

Why an electronic book?

We live in the Information Age—an exciting time in the history of human civilization, in which technology rules supreme and continues to progress in leaps and bounds every minute of every day. For a multitude of reasons, more and more avid literary fans are opting to purchase e-books instead of paper books. The question from those not yet initiated into the world of electronic reading is simply: *Why?*

1. ***Price.*** An electronic title at Ellora's Cave Publishing and Cerridwen Press runs anywhere from 40% to 75% less than the cover price of the exact same title in paperback format. Why? Basic mathematics and cost. It is less expensive to publish an e-book (no paper and printing, no warehousing and shipping) than it is to publish a paperback, so the savings are passed along to the consumer.

2. ***Space.*** Running out of room in your house for your books? That is one worry you will never have with electronic books. For a low one-time cost, you can purchase a handheld device specifically designed for e-reading. Many e-readers have large, convenient screens for viewing. Better yet, hundreds of titles can be stored within your new library—on a single microchip. There a variety of e-readers from different manufacturers. You can also read e-books on your PC or laptop computer. (Please note that Ellora's Cave does not endorse any specific brands.

You can check our websites at www.ellorascave.com or www.cerridwenpress.com for information we make available to new consumers.)

3. *Mobility.* Because your new e-library consists of only a microchip within a small, easily transportable e-reader, your entire cache of books can be taken with you wherever you go.

4. *Personal Viewing Preferences.* Are the words you are currently reading too small? Too large? Too... ANNOYING? Paperback books cannot be modified according to personal preferences, but e-books can.

5. *Instant Gratification.* Is it the middle of the night and all the bookstores near you are closed? Are you tired of waiting days, sometimes weeks, for bookstores to ship the novels you bought? Ellora's Cave Publishing sells instantaneous downloads twenty-four hours a day, seven days a week, every day of the year. Our webstore is never closed. Our e-book delivery system is 100% automated, meaning your order is filled as soon as you pay for it.

Those are a few of the top reasons why electronic books are replacing paperbacks for many avid readers.

As always, Ellora's Cave and Cerridwen Press welcome your questions and comments. We invite you to email us at Comments@ellorascave.com or write to us directly at Ellora's Cave Publishing Inc., 1056 Home Avenue, Akron, OH 44310-3502.

Cerridwen, the Celtic Goddess of wisdom, was the muse who brought inspiration to storytellers and those in the creative arts. Cerridwen Press encompasses the best and most innovative stories in all genres of today's fiction. Visit our site and discover the newest titles by talented authors who still get inspired - much like the ancient storytellers did, once upon a time.

Cerridwen Press
www.cerridwenpress.com